W9-BLD-300

ART2-D2'S

GUIDE TO FOLDING AND DOODLING

TOM ANGLEBERGER

AMULET BOOKS
NEW YORK

PUBLISHER'S NOTE: This is a work of fiction. Names, characters, places, and incidents are either the product of the author's imagination or are used fictitiously, and any resemblance to actual persons, living or dead, business establishments, events, or locales is entirely coincidental.

ISBN: 978-1-4197-0534-2

Text copyright © 2013 Tom Angleberger
Book design by Melissa J. Arnst

The cover and front matter illustrations are by Tom Angleberger and Jason Rosenstock. All other illustrations are by the author. The cover illustration and all other illustrations depicting R2-D2, C-3PO, Yoda, Darth Vader, Chewbacca, and all other Star Wars properties are copyright © 2013 Lucasfilm Ltd. Title and character and place names protected by all applicable trademark laws. All rights reserved. Used under authorization.

Published in 2013 by Amulet Books, an imprint of ABRAMS. All rights reserved. No portion of this book may be reproduced, stored in a retrieval system, or transmitted in any form or by any means, mechanical, electronic, photocopying, recording, or otherwise, without written permission from the publisher. Amulet Books and Amulet Paperbacks are registered trademarks of Harry N. Abrams, Inc.

Printed and bound in U.S.A.
10 9 8 7 6 5 4 3 2 1

Amulet Books are available at special discounts when purchased in quantity for premiums and promotions as well as fundraising or educational use. Special editions can also be created to specification. For details, contact specialsales@abramsbooks.com or the address below.

ABRAMS
THE ART OF BOOKS SINCE 1949
115 West 18th Street
New York, NY 10011
www.abramsbooks.com

THIS BOOK IS DEDICATED TO THE SUPERFOLDERS WHO HAVE SENT ME THEIR ORIGAMI, DRAWINGS, JOKES, MOVIES, AND CASE FILES. THANKS FOR ALL THE INSPIRATION! AND DON'T STOP . . . THIS WOULDN'T BE ANY FUN WITHOUT YOU!

CONTENTS

Art2-D2 and the New (Sort of) Case File, by Tommy 1
Beep! by Kellen 4

SECRETS OF THE JEDI SUPER DOODLERS

How to Draw Speedy Origami Yoda, by Kellen 10
How to Draw Speedy Origami Vader, by Kellen 12
How to Draw Speedy Fortune Wookiee, by Kellen 14
How to Draw Speedy Origami ART2-D2, by Kellen 16
How to Draw Un-turkeys, by Cassie 18
How to Draw Darth Vader's Helmet, by Kellen 22
Letter & Number Doodles, by Quavondo 24
Awesome Letters, by Remi 28
Tommy Can't Draw, by Tommy 34
Sara's Smiley Factory, by Sara 38
Lance's One-Liners, by Lance 42
How to Draw Dogs (and Cats), by Caroline 46
Caroline-Style *Star Wars* Creatures, by Kellen 50
Speech Balloons, by Kellen 56
Composition, by Kellen 58

ATTACK OF THE DOODLE-GAMI

Doodle-gami, by Dwight and Kellen 60
Universal Puppet, by Dwight and Kellen 67
Art2-D2 and C-3PO, by Dwight and Kellen 70
One More Fold, by Dwight and Kellen 73
Lastly . . . Lightsabers!, by Dwight and Kellen 75
Darth Paper, by Harvey and Kellen 76
Origami Yoda vs. Darth Paper, by Kellen 82
Kirigami General Grievous, by Dwight and Kellen 83

Origami Costumes, by Sara, Tommy, and Kellen 87
Folding 1,000 Yodas, by Origami Master Ben and Kellen 88
Don't Waste the Color Pages, by Kellen 89
Photographing Doodle-gami Puppets, by Rhondella 101

HOW TO DRAW PEOPLE

How to Draw Shirts and Pants, by Kellen 108
How to Draw Shoes, by Kellen 112
How to Draw Fake Hands & Arms, by Kellen 114
How to Draw Heads, by Kellen 116
How to Draw Eyes, by Kellen 118
How to Draw Faces, by Kellen 122
How to Draw Hands, by Kellen 126

MORE FUN!

Actual Bookmark 133
How to Talk Like Yoda, by Harvey 134
Trench Run: The 56¢ *Star Wars* Game, by Mike and Kellen 136
How to Make a Lip Balm Rocket, by Dwight and Kellen 138
How Dwight Fake-Cracks His Knuckles, by Tommy 140
How to Make Eraser Prints, by Murky and Kellen 141
Action Figure and Spaceship Prints, by Amy 144
Pencil Podracing, by Mike 148
How to Make Your Own Origami Yoda T-Shirt, by Kellen 154

The End Is the Beginning, by Tommy 158
Autobiography, by Harvey 160
Tommy and Kellen's Bibliography 164

ART2

ART2-D2 AND THE NEW (SORT OF) CASE FILE

BY TOMMY

Okay, so this case file is going to be really weird.

Well, I guess they've all been really weird, so maybe I should just say that this one is weird in a different way.

It all started when Kellen and Dwight came into the library one morning and asked me to help them make their own case file. Well, actually, Kellen was the one who asked. Dwight was trying to balance a pen on his nose. (His current record is one millisecond.)

"This is a million-dollar idea!" said Kellen. "I'm going to make a how-to case file of all of my secrets for being a master doodler . . ."

"A master doodler?" butted in Harvey. "A master drooler, yes. A master doodler . . . uh, no."

But Kellen kept going. "And Dwight's going to tell how to do origami. And Sara can do her smileys, and Murky makes that awesome Chewbacca stamp with an eraser. And everybody can put in something—even you, Tommy—and when we're done, we'll have this awesome case file full of doodling and folding and stuff, and maybe we can even get it published!"

"Published!?!?!?!" splurted Harvey. "You're not going to get it published. Who would want to buy a whole book full of junk like that?"

Dwight let the pen fall to the floor, and he held out Origami Yoda.

"So certain are you?" said Origami Yoda. "Always with you what cannot be done. This

case file . . . teach you what CAN be done it will."

"Sounds awesome," I said. "What should we call it? *Origami Yoda's Guide to Doodling, Folding, and Stuff*?"

"No," said Kellen. "Origami Yoda is going to help some, probably, but here's the star . . ."

And he pulled out this awesome Origami R2-D2. It was folded so that the dome was silver and the body was white.

"It's Art2-D2!" said Kellen.

Harvey's Comment

Somebody hide me until this is done.

Tommy's Comment: Aw, c'mon, Harvey. Give it a try. You might even become a Jedi Doodler.

Kellen's Comment

MORE LIKE A SITH SCRIBBLER . . . BUT ENOUGH YAKKING! LET'S GET TO WORK!

BEEP!
BY KELLEN
WHIRR... CLICK... BLIP!
WHAT DO YOU MEAN YOU CAN TEACH ANYBODY HOW TO DRAW?
BLRRR... CLICK...
EVEN HARVEY?
WE'RE DOOMED!

HA-HA! WELL, YOU ARE DOOMED! BECAUSE I CAN'T DRAW ANYTHING!
AND, FRANKLY, NEITHER CAN YOU, KELLEN! IS THAT SUPPOSED TO BE YOUR HAND?
K
H
HOW RUDE!
C'MON, HARVEY! WE'RE ALL GOING TO PUT TOGETHER A HOW-TO CASE FILE.
ALL RIGHT... ALL RIGHT... I'LL GIVE IT A TRY...
NO!
H

DOODLE OR DOODLE NOT! THERE IS NO TRY!
OH, GREAT! PAPERWAD YODA! WHAT IS HE DOING IN THIS CASE FILE?
HE'S HERE TO HELP YOU!
BUT HE'S NOT EVEN MAKING SENSE . . . AS USUAL!
YES, HE IS! THINK ABOUT IT!

SEE, THERE ARE NO RULES, REQUIREMENTS, GRADES, OR ANYTHING LIKE THAT FOR DOODLING. IF YOU'RE DOING IT . . . THEN YOU'RE DOING IT.
SCRIBBLE IN THIS BOX YOU MUST!
THE ONLY WAY YOU CAN FAIL IS BY NOT SCRIBBLING IN THE BOX. (YOU DID SCRIBBLE IN THE BOX, RIGHT?)
THAT'S DUMB! WHY SHOULD I SCRIBBLE IN THE BOX?
FIRST STEP IT IS IN JOURNEY TO BECOME A JEDI DOODLER.

BUT ALL I CAN DRAW ARE STICK FIGURES!
HARVEY
NO!
STICK FIGURES TO THE DARK SIDE ONLY LEAD!!!
HUH?
QUICKER, EASIER THEY ARE . . . BUT NOT WORTHY OF YOU . . .
COME, PADAWAN . . . LET US TEACH YOU . . .
WAIT A MINUTE! IS THIS GOING TO BE ONE OF THOSE THINGS WHERE I HAVE TO DRAW A BUNCH OF CIRCLES FIRST?
NO WAY . . . NO FANCY-PANTS STUFF . . . JUST GOOD OLD-FASHIONED DOODLING! LIKE THIS!
K
HEY! STOP DRAWING ME IN MY UNDERWEAR!
OKAY!
NOOO!
K
H

CHEETOS!
MOST IMPRESSIVE
SECRETS OF THE JEDI
ABE
FIZZ POP
SUPER DOODLERS
BEEP
CAD BANE
ROGER ROGER

HOW TO DRAW SPEEDY ORIGAMI YODA

BY KELLEN

I'VE HAD TO DRAW ORIGAMI YODA A MILLION TIMES. I FINALLY FIGURED OUT HOW TO DO IT IN ABOUT .8 SECONDS!

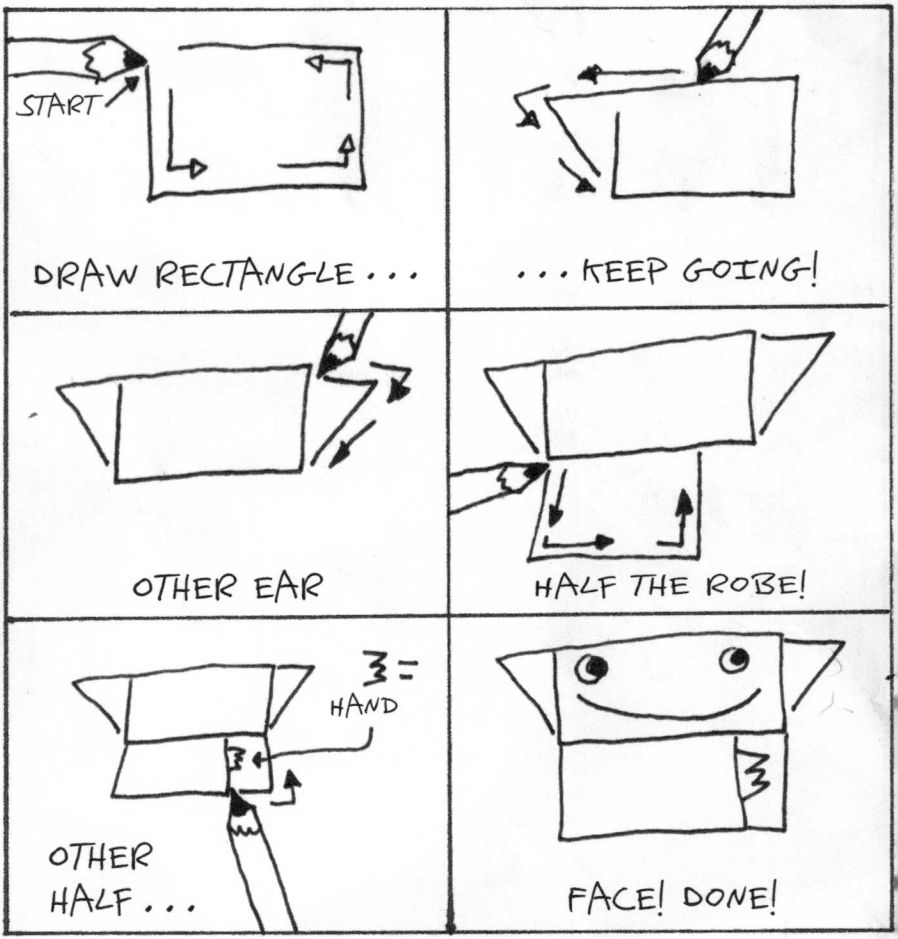

DRAW SOME GOOD ONES...

THEN DRAW SOME FAST ONES!

HOW TO DRAW SPEEDY ORIGAMI VADER

BY KELLEN

DARTH PAPER TAKES MORE LIKE 1.7 SECONDS, BUT HE'S STILL FAST!

HINT: DRAW RESPIRATOR LINES TO MAKE A FROWN . . . NOT A SMILE!

DRAW VADER . . .

NOW YOU CAN MAKE THEM FIGHT!

HOW TO DRAW SPEEDY FORTUNE WOOKIEE

BY KELLEN

WITH CHEWIE, THE FASTER YOU DRAW HIM, THE MORE WOOKIEE-ISH HE LOOKS!

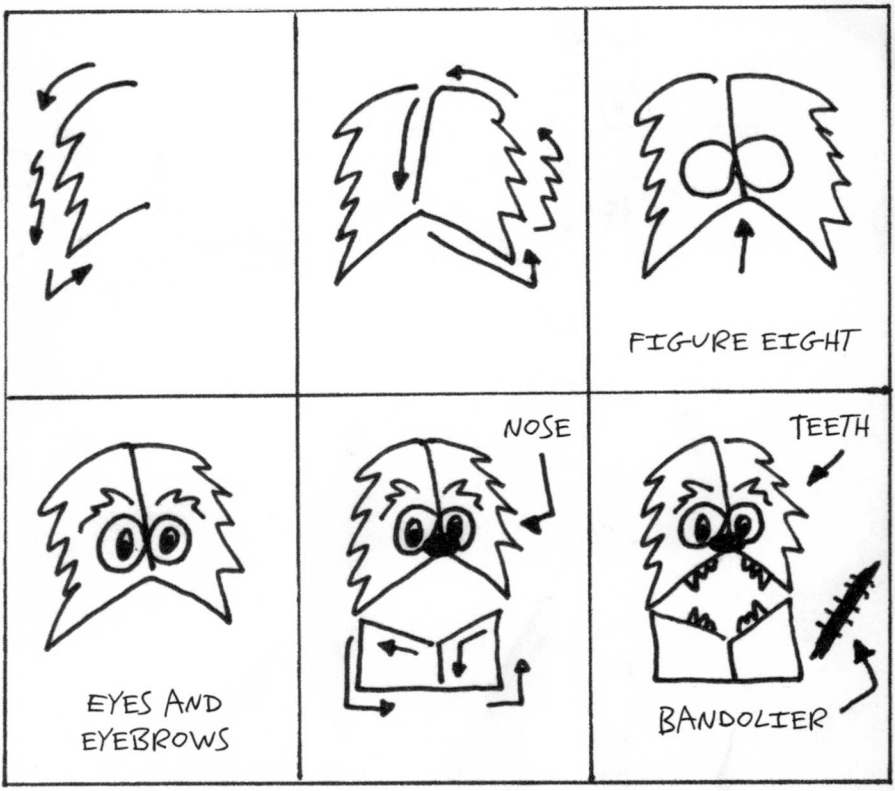

CHEWIE'S BANDOLIER IS JUST A THICK LINE WITH FOUR OR FIVE LINES ACROSS IT. TECHNICALLY, IT SHOULD REALLY BE A THICK BLACK STRIPE WITH TINY WHITE RECTANGLES ON IT, BUT THAT IS A PAIN TO DRAW.

TRY SOME CHEWIES HERE...

HOW TO DRAW SPEEDY ORIGAMI ART2-D2

BY KELLEN

ART2'S BODY IS EASY BUT THE DROID BITS TAKE A LITTLE EXTRA TIME.

HOW ABOUT SOME ARTS?

HOW TO DRAW UN-TURKEYS

BY CASSIE

Hi, I'm Cassie! I'm going to teach you how to draw an Imperial AT-AT

Just turn your hand outline upside down. Add some details and . . .

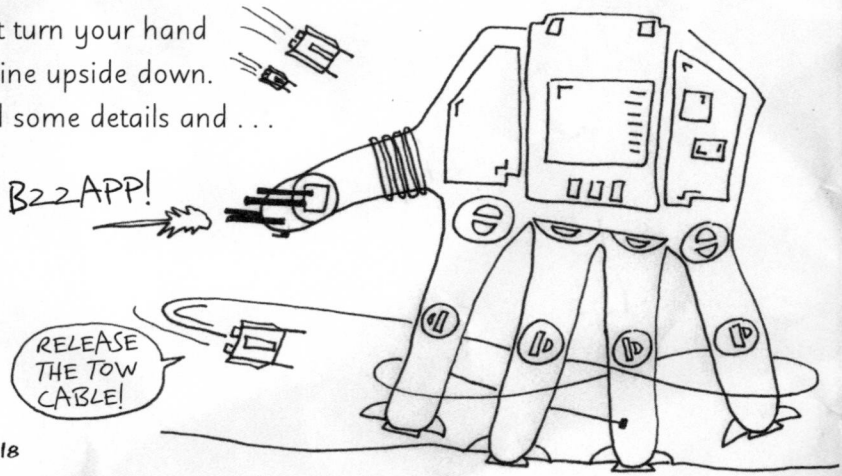

Turn the book sideways
and trace your hand here . . .

What other un-turkeys can you make? How about Modal Nodes?

Try it on this hand, and then try it with your own hand!

Trace your hand again here . . .

HOW TO DRAW DARTH VADER'S HELMET

BY KELLEN

YOUR TURN. (TRY NOT TO LET HIS HELMET GET LUMPY! HE HATES THAT!)

LETTER & NUMBER DOODLES

BY QUAVONDO

SOMETIMES GETTING STARTED HARDEST PART CAN BE . . .

BLANK PAGE . . . FRIGHTENING IT CAN BE.

That's why I like to start with letters and numbers!

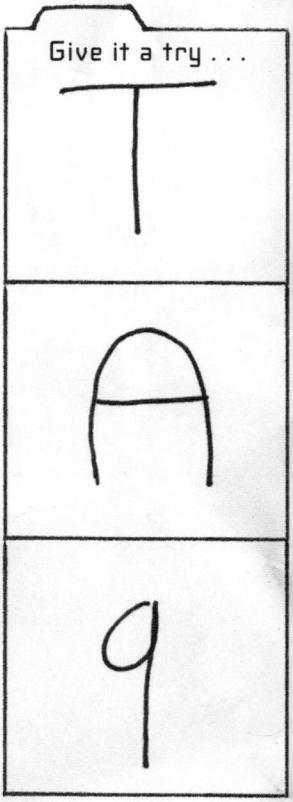

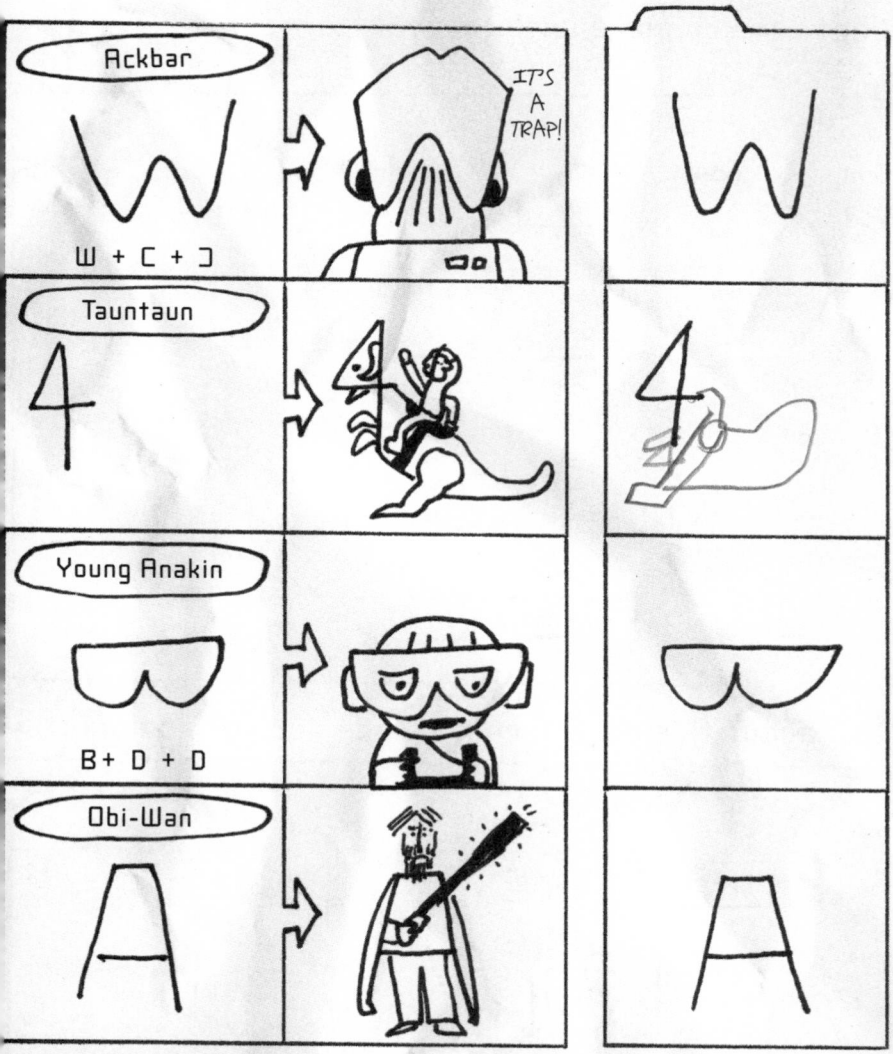

What else can you make?

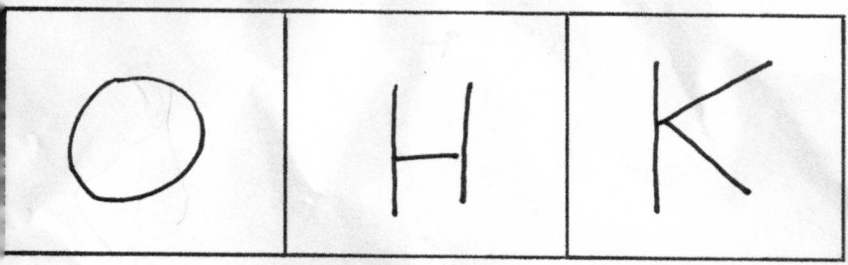

What can you make with these letters?

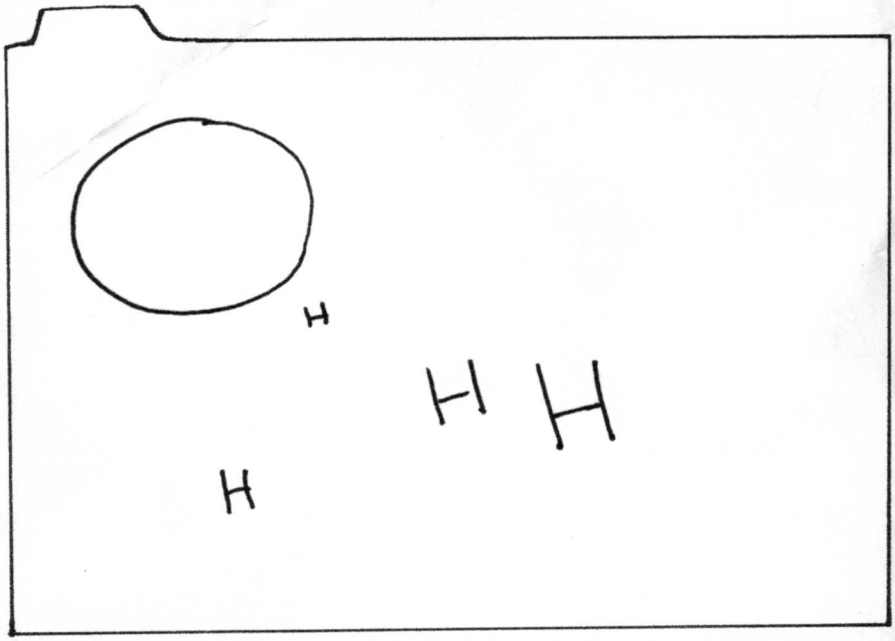

How about this one? Turn it upside down if you want!

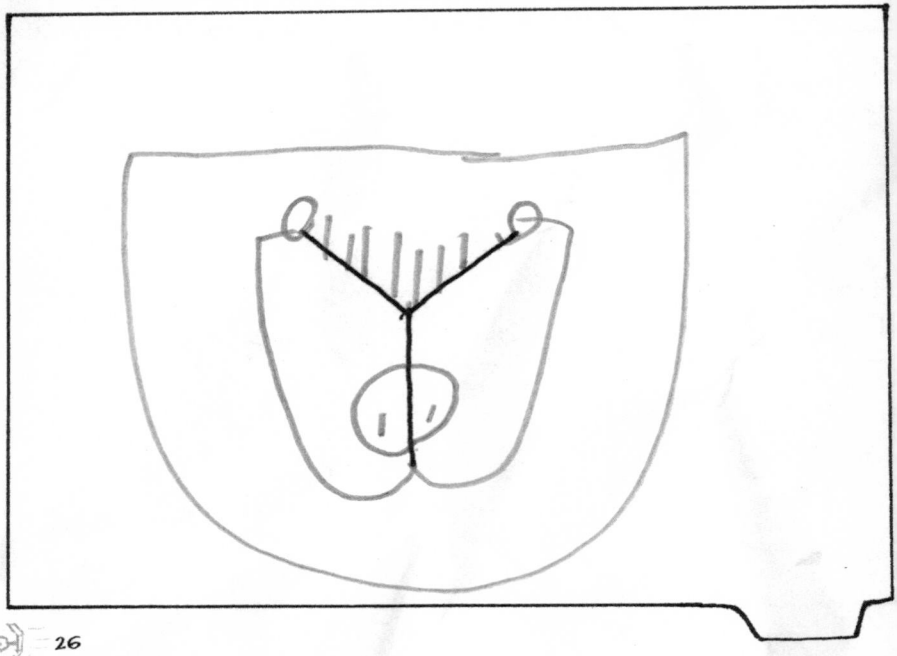

Try your own . . .

AWESOME LETTERS

BY REMI (WITH INTRODUCTION BY KELLEN)

CAN YOU IMAGINE IF THE STAR WARS LOGO LOOKED LIKE THE ONE ON THE LEFT???? OF COURSE NOT!! GEORGE LUCAS CARES ABOUT MAKING THINGS LOOK GOOD, SO HE HIRED AN ARTIST TO MAKE THE AWESOMEST, STOOKIEST TITLE EVER...

WELL, I WANTED TO BE ABLE TO MAKE COOL LETTERS LIKE THAT, TOO... THAT'S WHY I CALLED AN EXPERT... THE QUEEN OF BOOK COVER DOODLING...

Okay, first thing to do is to learn to draw around regular letters, like this . . .

Try it . . .

S W Q ?

That was mega easy, right? Well, if you practice a bit, it will get just as easy to draw the outlines without drawing the regular letters first!!!

Just IMAGINE you are drawing around the regular letters, okay?

Note: Try to get the holes in the right places.

NO NO YES

(Unless you WANT it that way.)

3D

3-D letters are easy! Or at least not TOO hard! Let's start super easy with "L" . . .

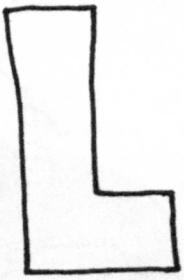

Start with outline.

Draw diagonal lines at corners.

Connect the ends of the lines with more lines. And then shade.

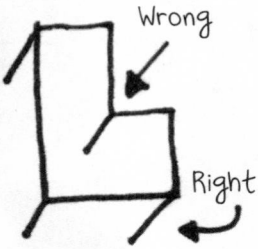

Don't draw the diagonal lines over the top of your letter. And make sure they all slant the same way.

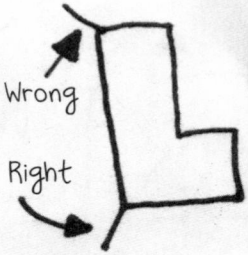

Try with these outlines . . .

Some letters are harder than others . . . especially round ones! Don't worry about getting them perfect.

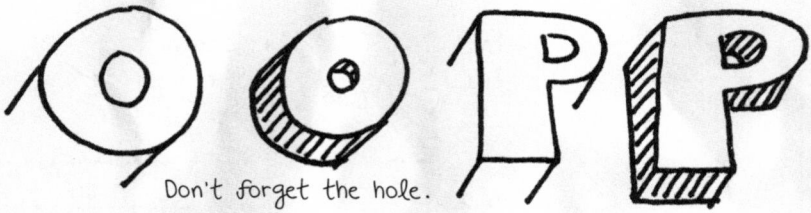

Practice your letters here:

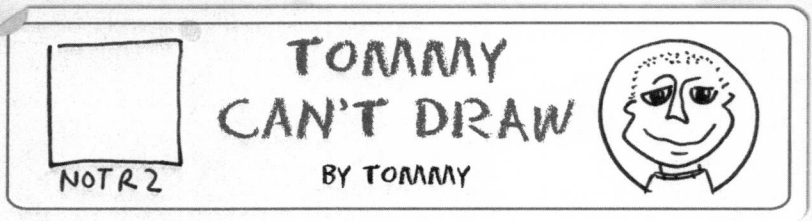

I'm really hoping this case file helps me learn how to draw, because I stink right now. But I still wanted to be part of the case file! Then I remembered these drawings I saw somewhere.

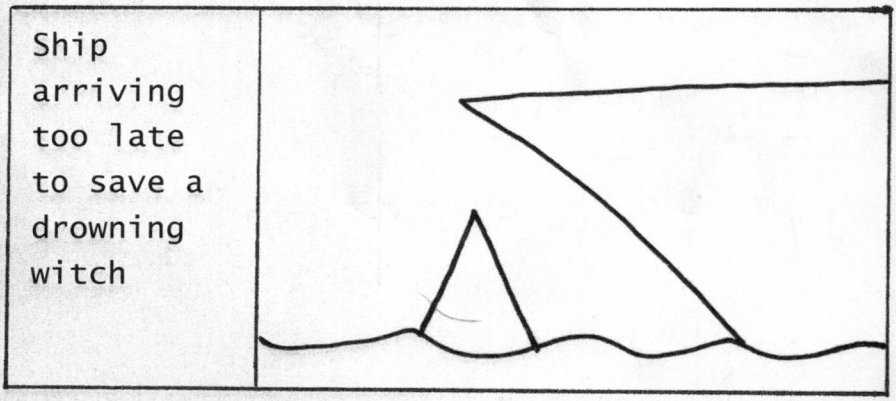

You can draw that drawing without knowing how to draw! So I realized it would be easy to change it over to Star Wars . . .

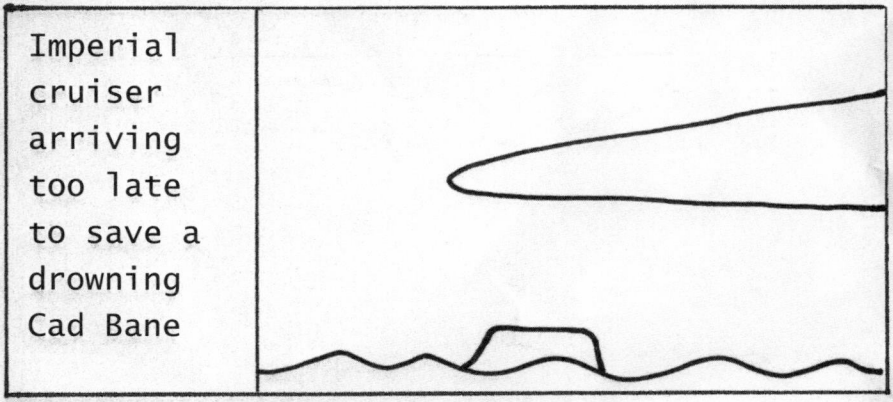

See if you can guess what these are:

1.

2.

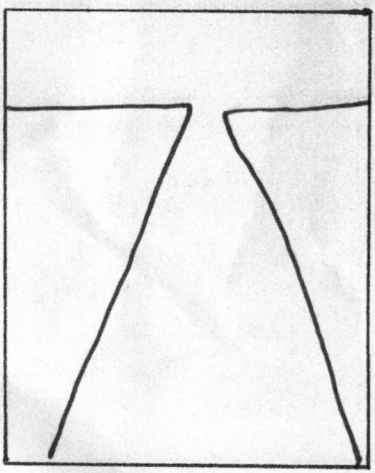

3.

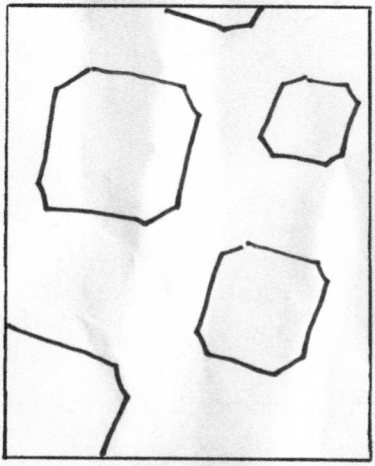

4.

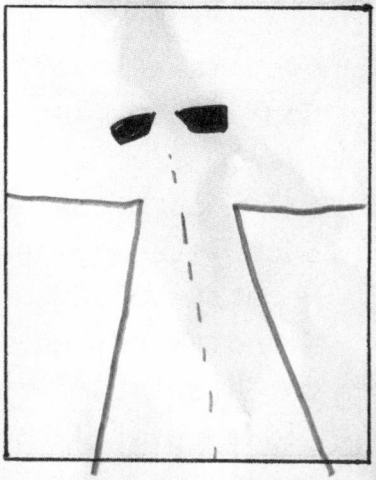

5.

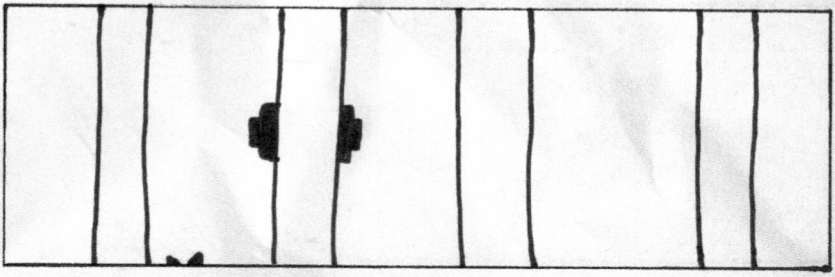

(Turn the page for answers.)

Answers

1. "Put down that X-wing, Yoda!"
2. Too close to a clone, or two sandcrawlers about to bump into each other.
3. TIE fighter attack!! From the side!!
4. Snowtrooper in a snowstorm, or two sandcrawlers about to bump into each other . . . in a sandstorm.
5. Wicket finds Princess Leia hiding in a forest on Endor.

Can you make some?

1. Gonk droid (leg-only view)
2. Close-up of Sy Snootles singing
3. Mace Windu and Ki-Adi-Mundi go for a swim.
4. Close-up of Jabba's tongue.
5. Grievous's cape . . . on a clothesline
6. Make up your own!

1.

2.

3.

4.

5.

6.

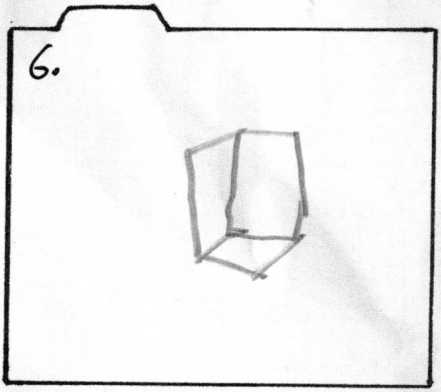

SARA'S SMILEY FACTORY
BY SARA
Trace a quarter
Add details
HI! I'M LEIA!
Just a few details will do it!
LUKE
HAN
OBI-WAN
Try here:
UH, WHY IS EVERYBODY SMILING?
BECAUSE THEY'RE SMILEYS! DUH!

DWIGHT
TOMMY
KELLEN
RHONDELLA
Your friends here:
AMY
SNICKERS
MURKY

Leaving gaps can be useful . . .

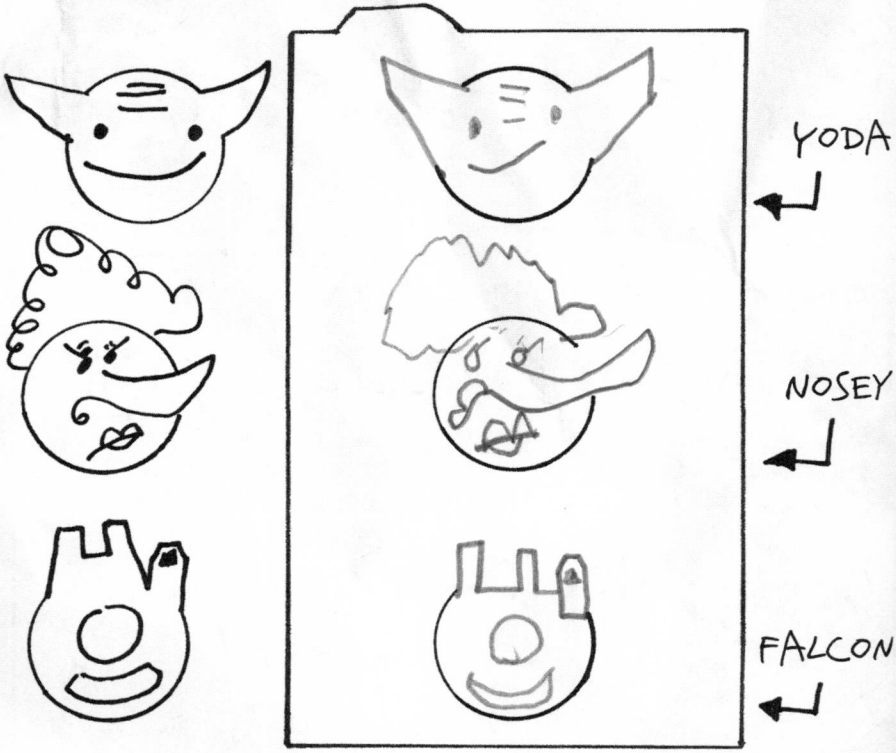

It's all about eye placement!

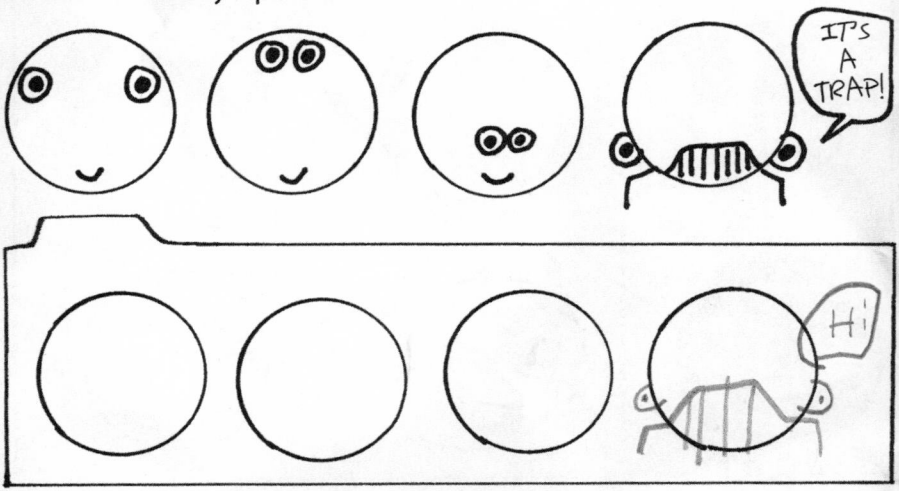

Trace top of quarter.
Add a square bottom.
BOBA
BANTHA
JABBA
CANTINA DUDE
YOU'RE RIGHT, ARTZ. NOT EVERYONE SHOULD BE A SMILEY!

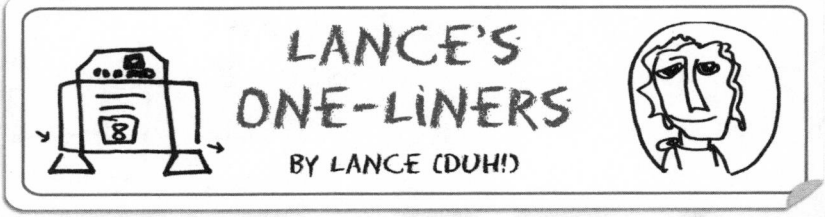

Don't tell Yoda, but these are almost as easy to draw as stick figures! And they are quicker because you don't lift up your pen (much). Just let it flow!

Here's a Basic Dude:

Practice the basic dude a couple times . . . then try variations!

Believe it or not, you can draw Jabba with ONE line! (Well, plus two eyes and maybe Bib Fortuna and Salacious Crumb.)

Don't worry, Art2. I didn't forget you!

HOW TO DRAW DOGS (AND CATS)

BY CAROLINE

You can draw most of a dog with a single line. Like this . . .

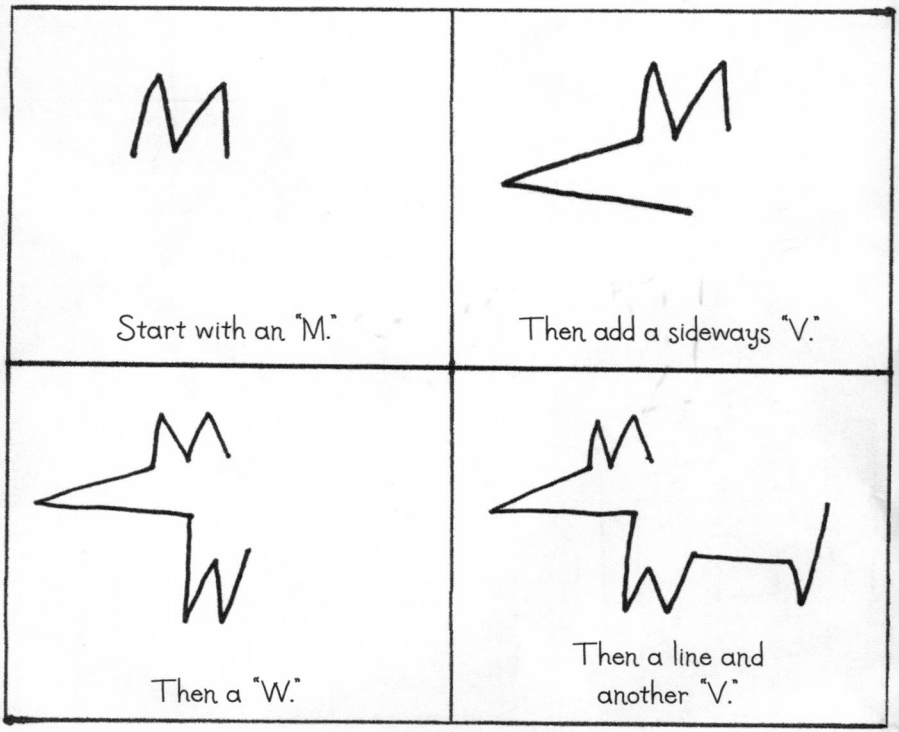

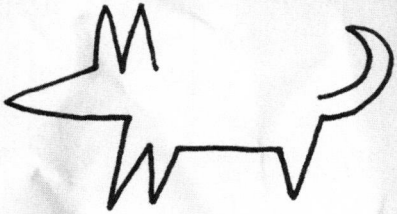

Add any kind of tail you want.

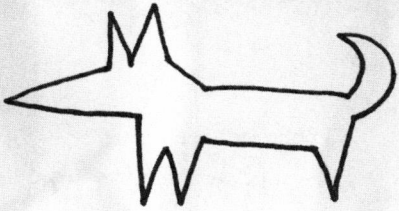

Then draw a line over and up to connect with the ears.

Add dots for the eyes and nose and a thick line for a collar.

Add a mouth and a "V" for the back leg.

Now that you can draw a basic dog, add details to make better dogs!

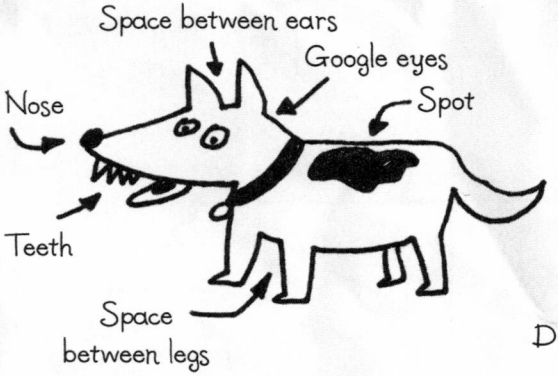

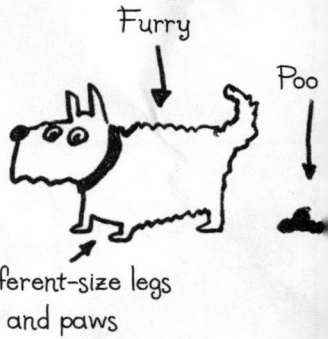

You can draw cats the same way!!

CAROLINE-STYLE STAR WARS CREATURES

BY KELLEN

HERE'S HOW TO USE CAROLINE'S TECHNIQUE TO MAKE THE AWESOME ARENA BEAST, REEK!

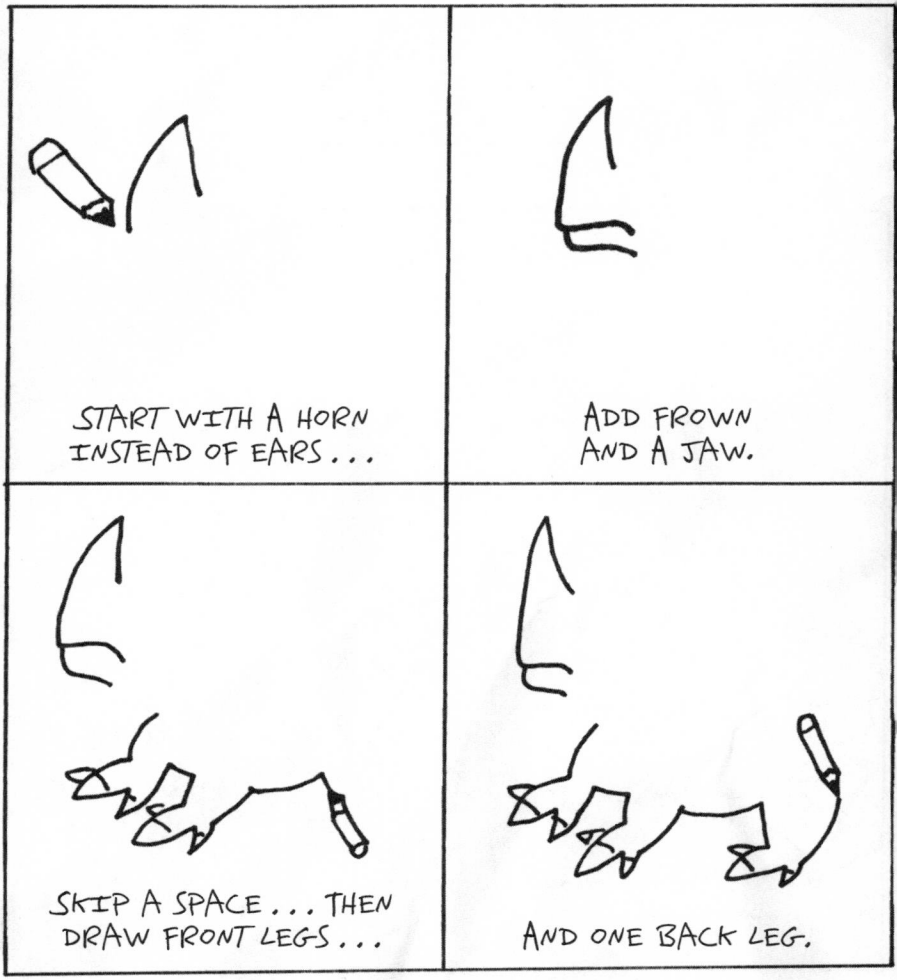

ADD STUMPY TAIL AND LUMPY, HUMPY BACK. CONNECT TO NOSE.

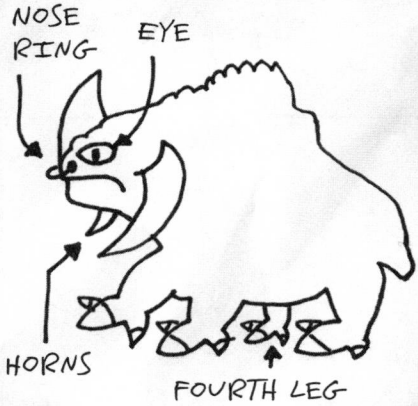

FILL IN DETAILS...

OR AN AT-AT!

DWARF
SPIDER
DROID

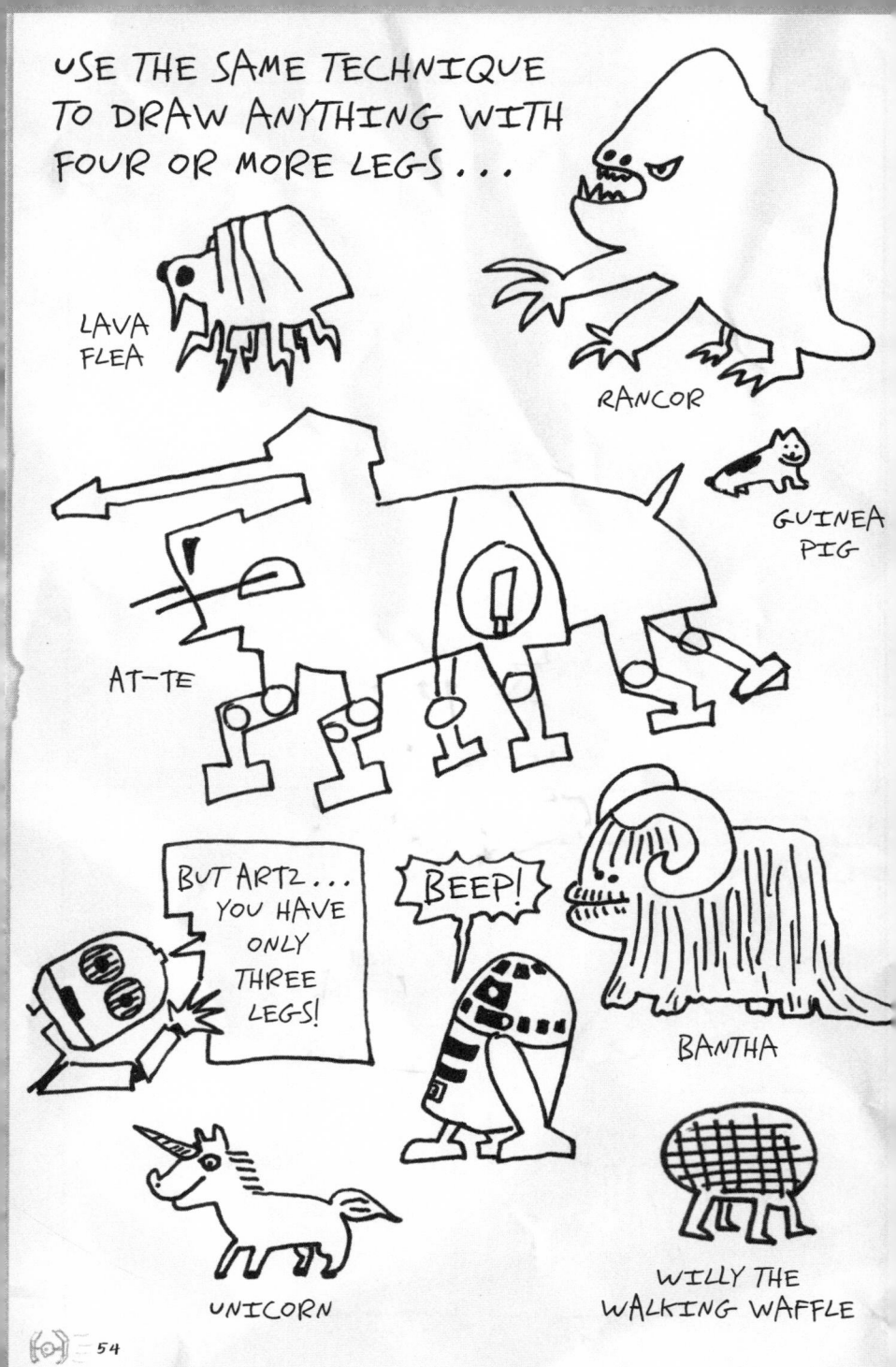
USE THE SAME TECHNIQUE TO DRAW ANYTHING WITH FOUR OR MORE LEGS...
LAVA FLEA
RANCOR
GUINEA PIG
AT-TE
BUT ARTZ... YOU HAVE ONLY THREE LEGS!
BEEP!
BANTHA
UNICORN
WILLY THE WALKING WAFFLE

DRAW YOUR OWN CREATURES...

SPEECH BALLOONS

BY KELLEN

ONCE YOU START DRAWING CHARACTERS OR CREATURES, YOU'RE GOING TO WANT TO MAKE THEM TALK BY ADDING A SPEECH BALLOON. I DON'T MEAN TO SOUND LIKE HARVEY, BUT... DO IT RIGHT!

BEFORE DRAWING SPEECH BALLOON, WORDS YOU MUST FIRST WRITE!

BEFORE DRAWING SPEECH BALLOON, WORDS YOU MUST FIRST WRITE!

MUST!

BEFORE DRAWING SPEECH BALLOON, WORDS YOU MUST FIRST WRITE!
PROVE IT TO YOURSELF . . .
WHICH IS EASIER, TRYING TO CRAM ALL THESE WORDS INTO A PRE-DRAWN SPEECH BALLOON . . .
OR JUST DRAWING A BALLOON AROUND PRE-WRITTEN WORDS?
REMEMBER . . .
THOUGHTS GO IN BUBBLES, NOT BALLOONS.

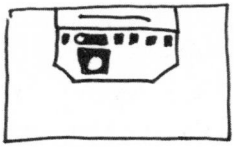

COMPOSITION

BY KELLEN

A LOT OF THE TIME WHEN YOU'RE DOODLING, YOU HAVE TO CRAM IN YOUR DRAWINGS WHEREVER YOU CAN. BUT IF YOU'VE GOT A BUNCH OF SPACE TO FILL, TRY TO DO IT WITH STYLE...

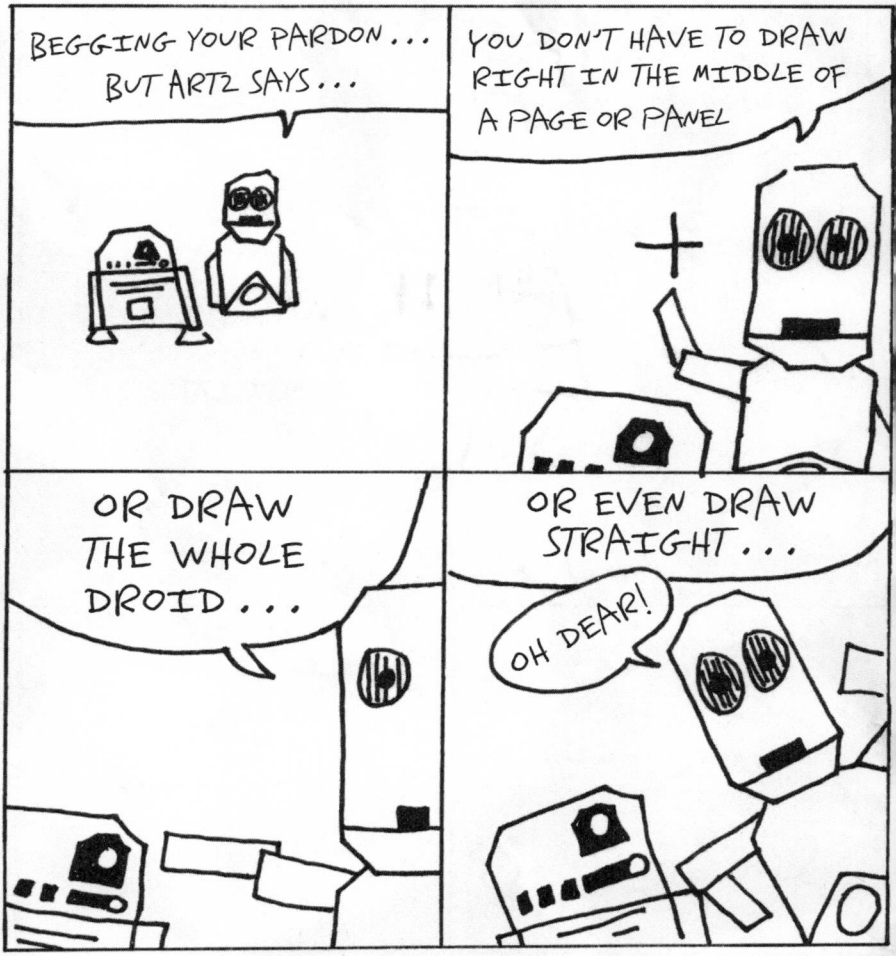

NOW IT'S DWIGHT'S TURN . . .

DOODLE-GAMI
BY DWIGHT AND KELLEN
39¢
DWIGHT MAKES THE ORIGAMI.
+
KELLEN MAKES THE DOODLES.
TOGETHER THEY MAKE... DOODLE-GAMI!!!
DOODLE-GAMI? SERIOUSLY?
YES! NOW HUSH UP, CUT A PIECE OF PAPER INTO FOUR PIECES, AND START FOLDING!
1 2
3 4

FIRST, DWIGHT WILL SHOW US HOW TO MAKE THE WORLD'S SIMPLEST FINGER PUPPET! JUST THREE FOLDS!

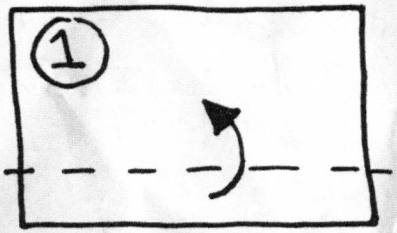

FOLD UP.

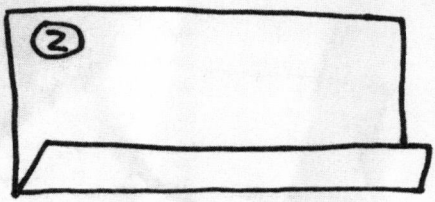

FLIP OVER.

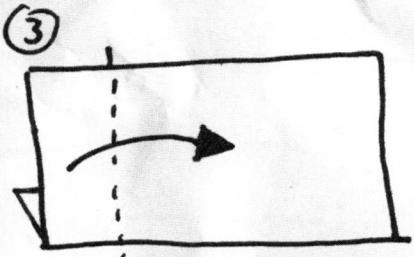

FOLD OVER.

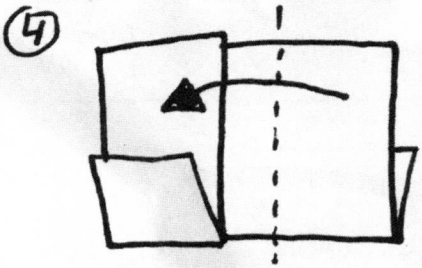

FOLD OVER.

LIFT UP FLAP A AND TUCK FLAP B INSIDE...

TRICKY AT FIRST, BUT YOU'LL GET IT!

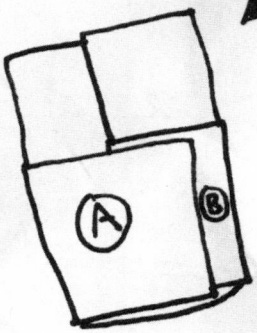

THIS LOCKS THE PUPPET TOGETHER FOR ADDED PUPPETABILITY!

TURN THE PAGE.

FLIP PUPPET OVER. NOW YOU HAVE A BLANK PUPPET THAT YOU CAN TURN INTO ALMOST ANYBODY BY DOODLING ON IT!

HINT: PRACTICE YOUR DOODLE FIRST, BEFORE YOU DRAW ON THE FINGER PUPPET!

DRAW ANYBODY AND THEN MAKE THEM SAY ANYTHING!

HOW DO YOU LIKE MY UNDER-PANTS?

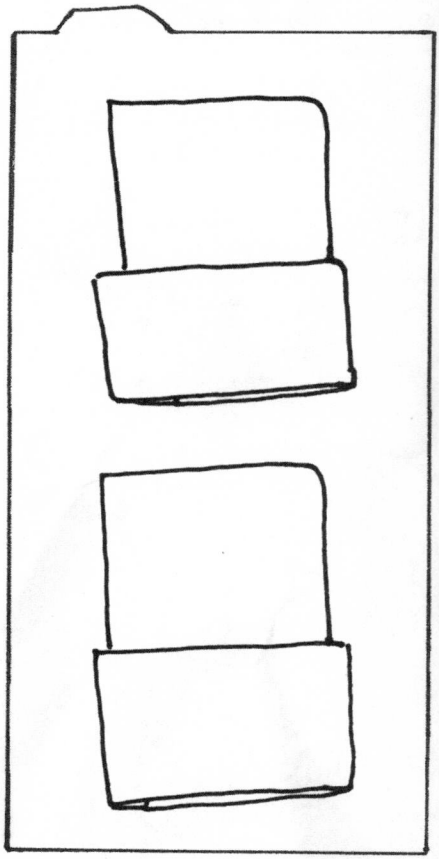

NOW TRY SOME EASY VARIATIONS TO GET DIFFERENT PUPPETS. START WITH PAPER TALL INSTEAD OF SHORT.

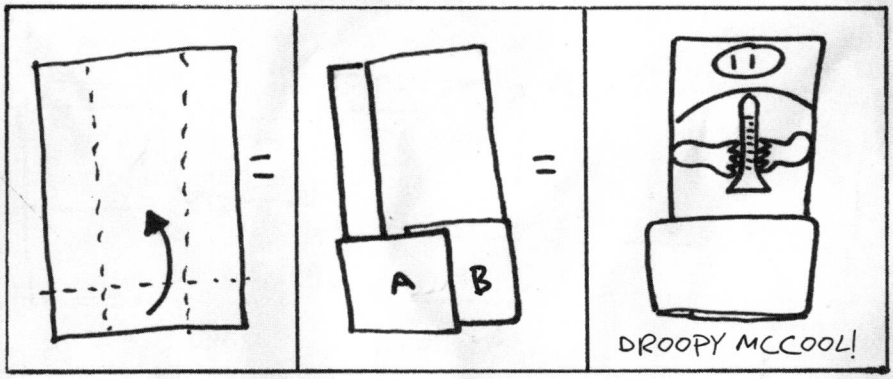

OR TRY MAKING FOLD 1 BIGGER . . .

OR BEND CORNERS DOWN TO ROUND HEAD.

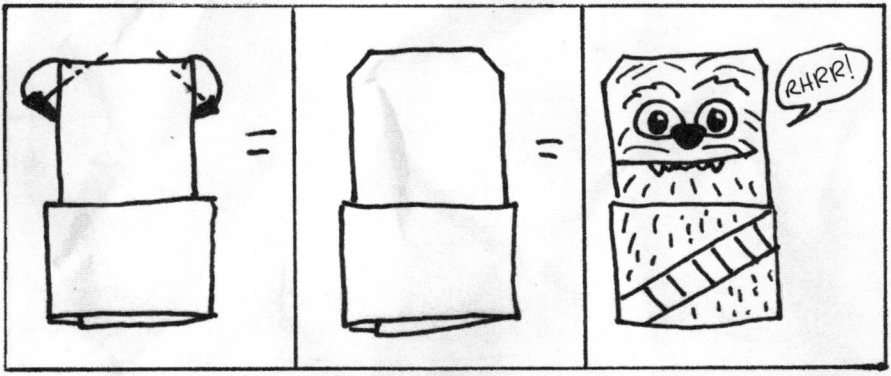

HERE'S A HAIRY VARIATION!

BETWEEN STEPS 1 AND 2, ADD A FOLD OR TWO TO CREATE HAIR . . .

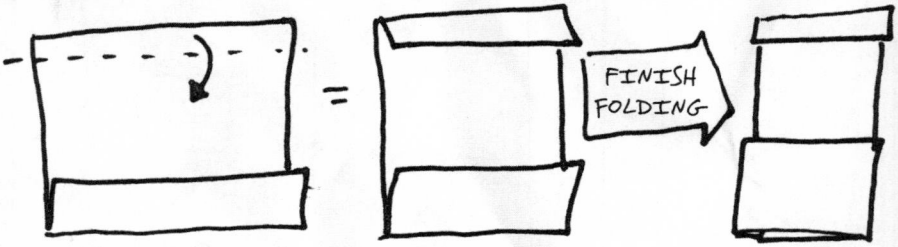

— OR —

FINISH FOLDING AND PULL EXTRA PAPER FROM BACK FOR HAIR.

AND HERE'S AN IMPERIAL VARIATION! STORMTROOPERS AND CLONE TROOPERS!

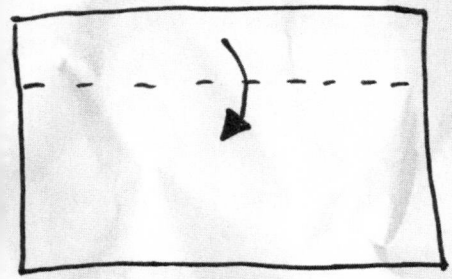

FOLD DOWN.

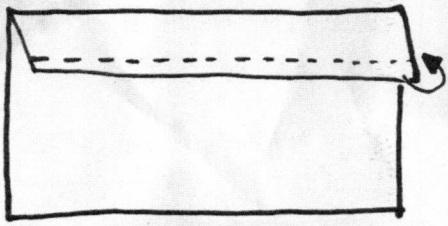

FOLD UP A THIN STRIP.

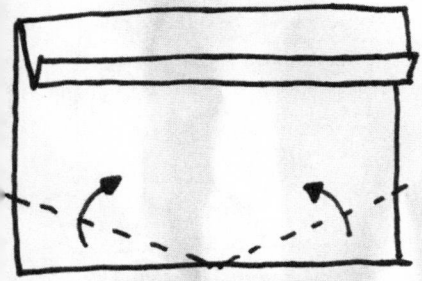

FOLD UP CORNERS.

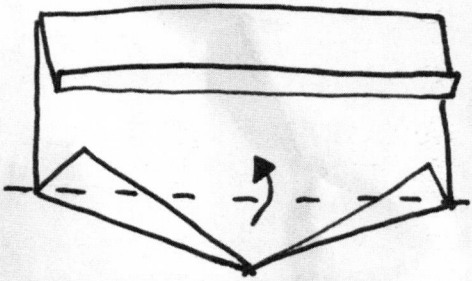

FOLD POINT UP.

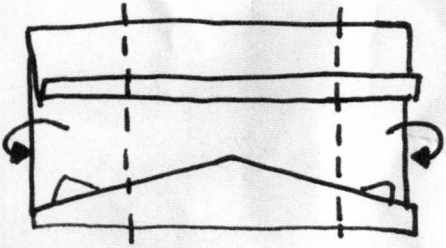

NOW FOLD SIDES BACK LIKE WITH THE BASIC PUPPET. (BUT DON'T TUCK FLAPS YET!)

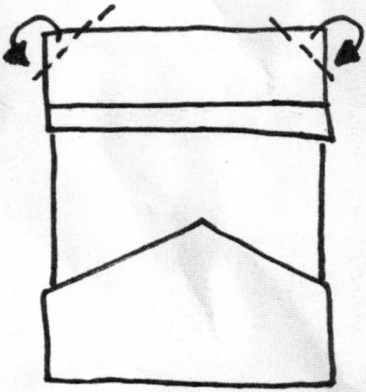

FOLD BACK CORNERS TO MAKE HELMET ROUND.

OPTIONAL!!!
USE YOUR INDEX FINGER TO PULL PAPER FROM BEHIND THE HELMET.
INSERT FINGER BEHIND HELMET . . .
PULL OUT A SMALL POCKET TO EXTEND HELMET SIDES . . .
COLOR THIS WHOLE STRIP.
EYES ARE ROUNDED TRIANGLES.
MAKE A TRIANGLE ABOVE FLAP, THEN FILL WITH THICK LINES. (MOVE FLAP TO MAKE DRAWING EASIER.)
DON'T FORGET THIS STUFF.
WITH SOME TWEAKS YOU CAN MAKE CLONES!
PHASE II
REX
BUT MAKE SURE YOU GET THEIR MARKINGS RIGHT!

UNIVERSAL PUPPET

BY DWIGHT AND KELLEN

YOU CAN MAKE THIS PUPPET INTO ALMOST ANYTHING . . . DEPENDING ON HOW YOU START.

TURN YOUR PAPER EITHER . . .

SHORT (LIKE ART2-D2)

OR

TALL (LIKE C-3PO)

EITHER WAY, THE FOLDS ARE BASICALLY THE SAME . . . LET'S START WITH SHORT!

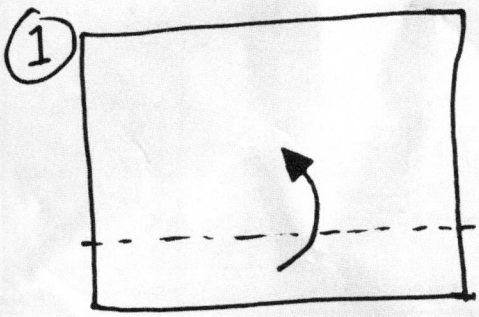

YOU CAN EXPERIMENT WITH WHERE YOU MAKE THIS FOLD . . .

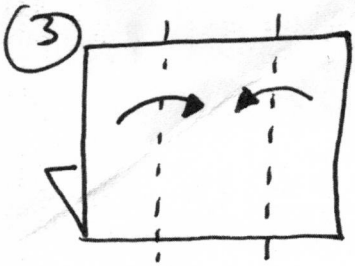
3

4
FOLD FLAP OUT.
DON'T FOLD THIS.

5
FOLD FLAP OUT.

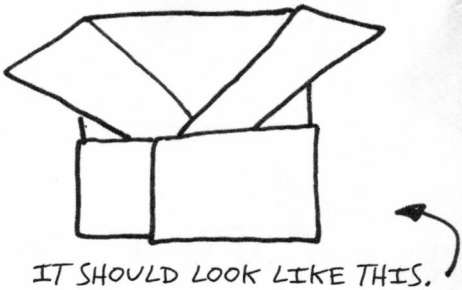
IT SHOULD LOOK LIKE THIS.

6
TUCK FLAPS LIKE ON PAGE 61.

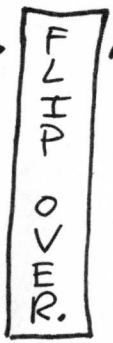
FLIP OVER.

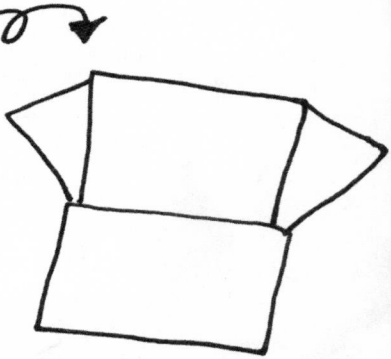

UH... WHAT IS IT?
IT'S ANYTHING YOU WANT TO MAKE IT!
EVEN ME!

BY MESSING WITH THE EARFLAPS, TWEAKING THE FOLDS, AND DOODLING, YOU CAN MAKE THE UNIVERSAL PUPPET INTO (ALMOST) ANYBODY!

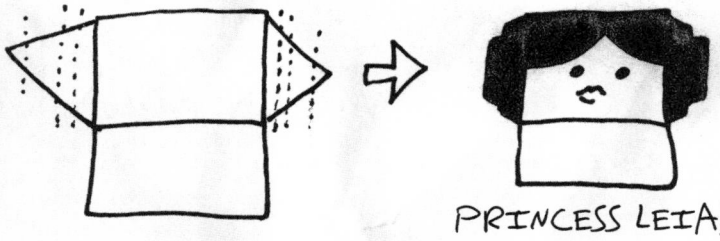

DON'T BE AFRAID TO **EXPERIMENT!**

ART2-D2 AND C-3PO

BY DWIGHT AND KELLEN

YOU CAN USE THE UNIVERSAL TECHNIQUE TO MAKE BOTH DROIDS! FIRST: ART2!

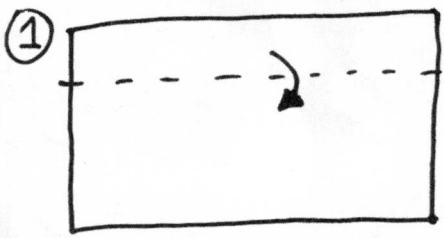

FOLD TOP DOWN. (NOT TOO FAR!)

FLIP OVER.

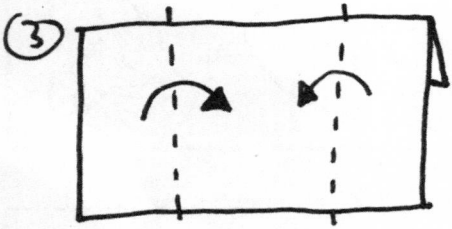

FOLD BOTH SIDES OVER.

4

INSTEAD OF FOLDING THE TOP CORNERS OUT, WE'LL USE THE BOTTOM CORNERS HERE . . .

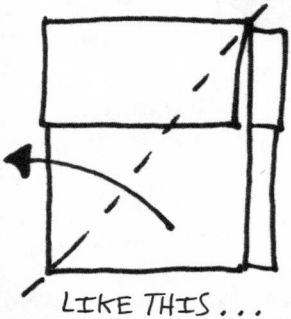

LIKE THIS . . .

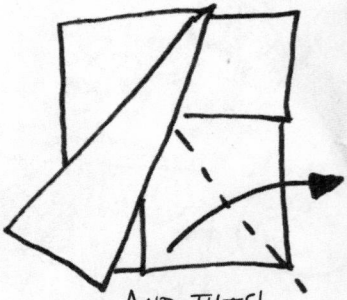

AND THIS!

(NOTE: DOTTED LINE GOES FROM CORNER TO CORNER.)

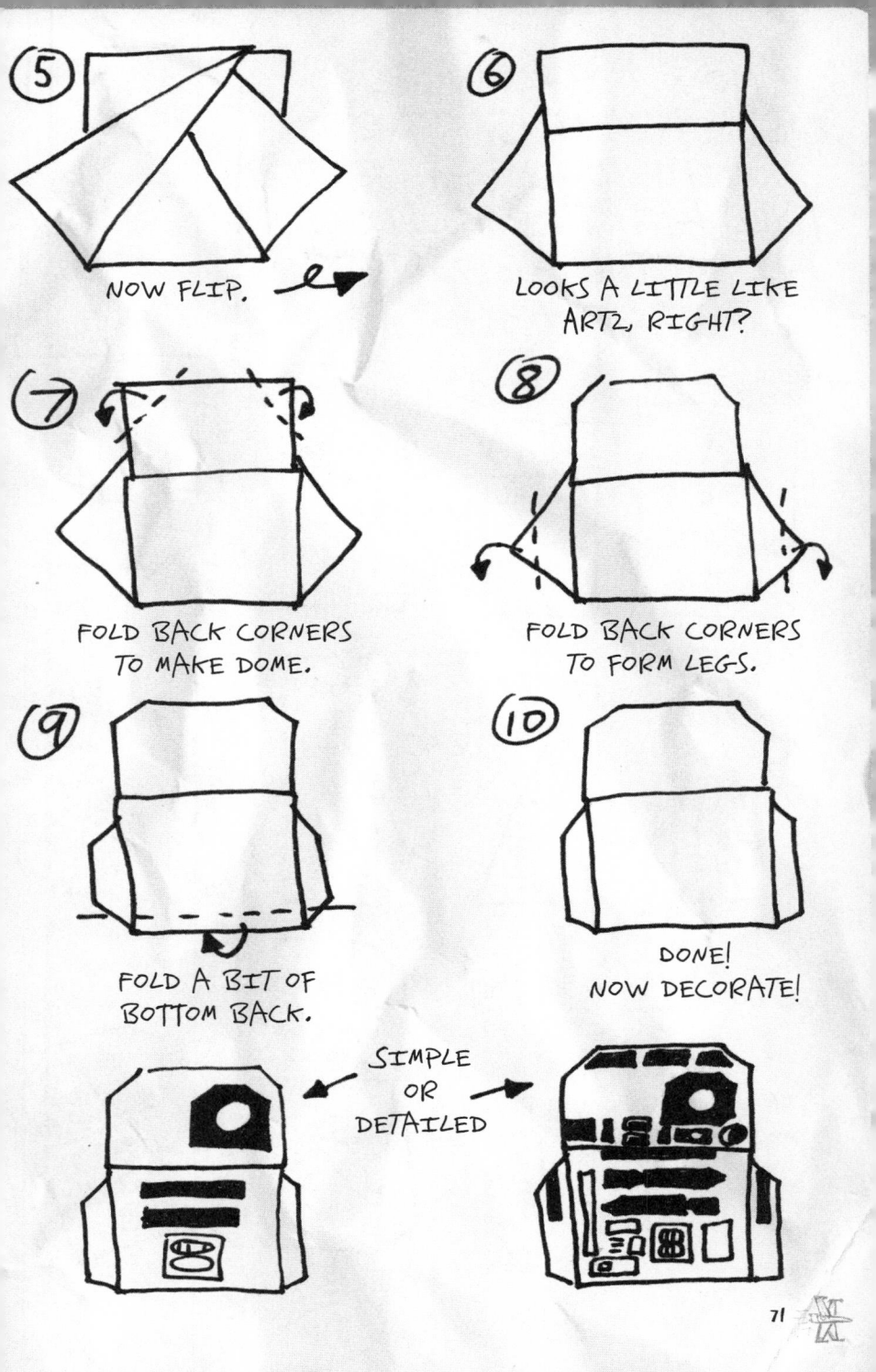
5
NOW FLIP.
6
LOOKS A LITTLE LIKE ART2, RIGHT?
7
FOLD BACK CORNERS TO MAKE DOME.
8
FOLD BACK CORNERS TO FORM LEGS.
9
FOLD A BIT OF BOTTOM BACK.
10
DONE! NOW DECORATE!
SIMPLE OR DETAILED

NOW C-3PO WILL BE EASY! JUST START WITH YOUR PAPER TALL AND THEN FOLLOW ALL OF THE ART2 STEPS EXCEPT #9.

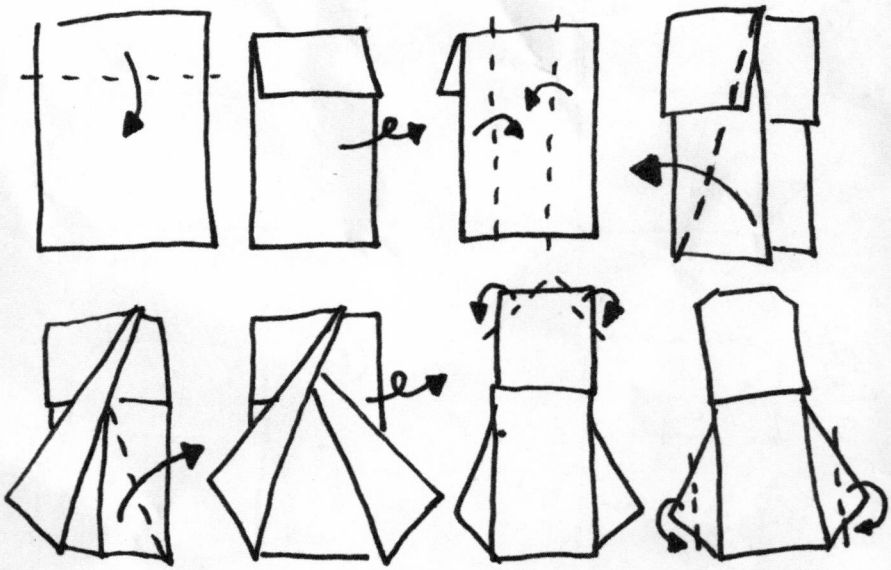

NOW DECORATE!

HINT: EYES ARE CIRCLE + LINES + A DOT.

ONE MORE FOLD

BY DWIGHT AND KELLEN

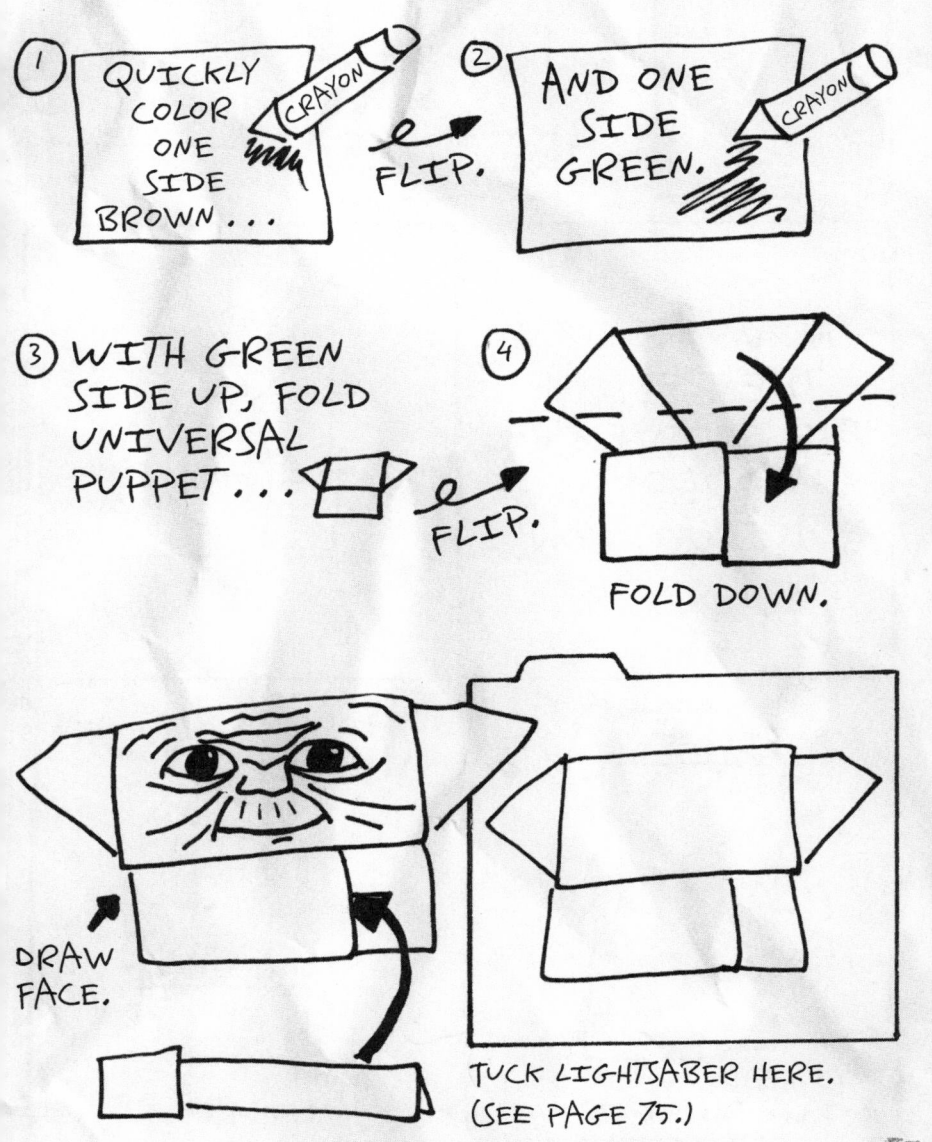

OR . . . TRY TALL! LEAVE ONE SIDE WHITE. COVER THE OTHER WITH ORANGE DOTS.

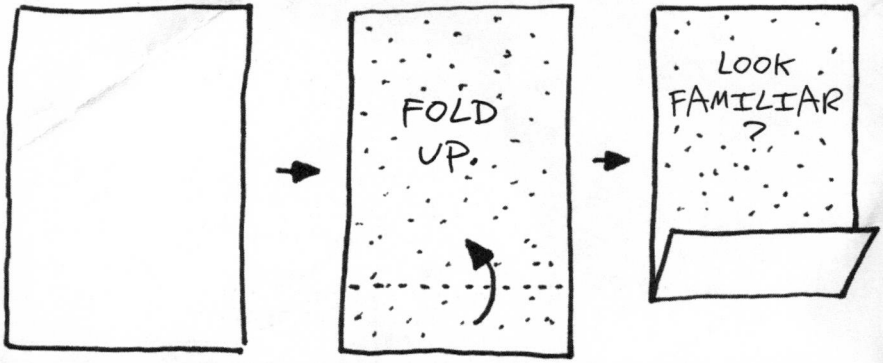

NOW FOLLOW THE REST OF THE UNIVERSAL PUPPET INSTRUCTIONS.

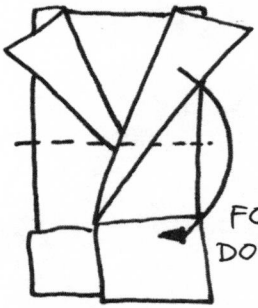

YOU SHOULD HAVE SOMETHING LIKE THIS . . .

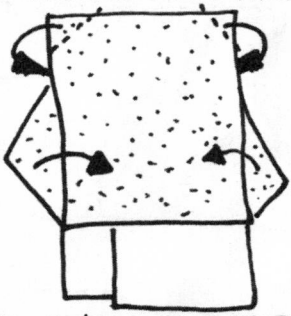

FOLD HEAD CORNERS BACK AND EYE TRIANGLES OVER.

ADD EYES, MOUTH, UNIFORM STUFF.

LASTLY . . . LIGHTSABERS!

BY DWIGHT AND KELLEN

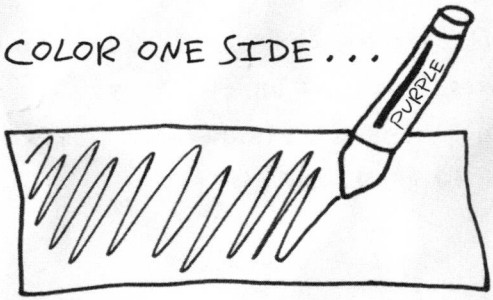

NOW FINISH LIKE A THREE-FOLD PUPPET!

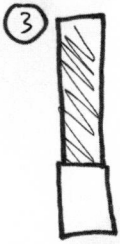

NICE AND STURDY

D SWITCHES
'D DIALS ON
HANDLE
OR COLOR
BLACK.

READY FOR ACTION!

DARTH PAPER

INVENTED BY HARVEY
DRAWN BY KELLEN

At last! I, Harvey, will finally reveal how to fold Darth Paper! Not Ben's Darth Paper (which I admit was pretty good) but MY Darth Paper! The REAL Darth Paper! But it's not easy! This is advanced stuff. First make sure you know how to make a pleat . . .

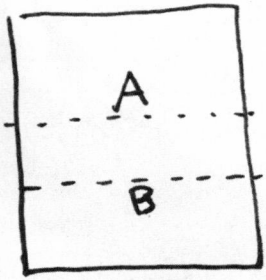

How to pleat

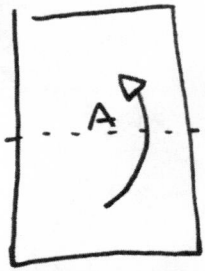

Fold up on A . . .

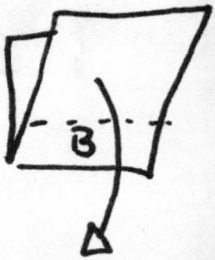

and down on B.

Result: a paper zigzag!

Side view

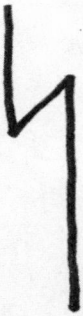

Okay . . . ready for Darth?

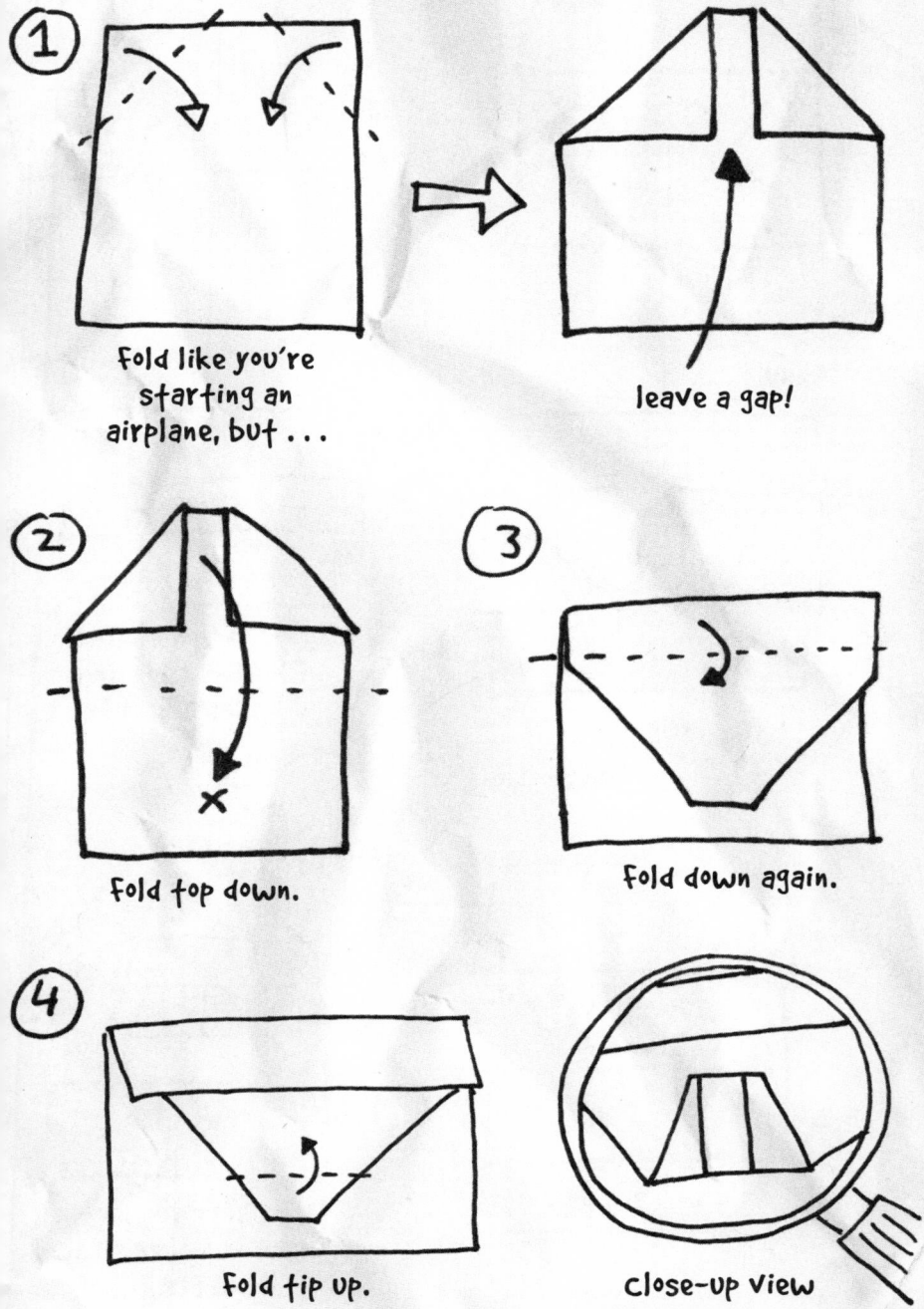

5 Here comes the pleat!

Fold up on A . . .

6

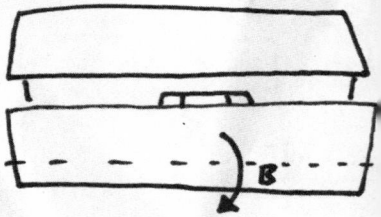

and down on B.

Result . . .

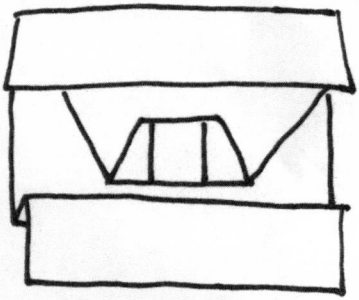

Right!

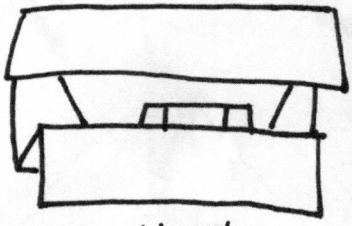

Wrong!
Pleat is covering
Vader's face!

7

Fold corners down to
make helmet sides.

Result

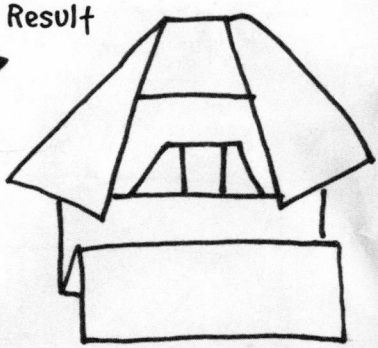

Make sure you haven't
covered Vader's face!
(He hates that!)

(8) This is a hard fold, because you have to bend many layers of paper!

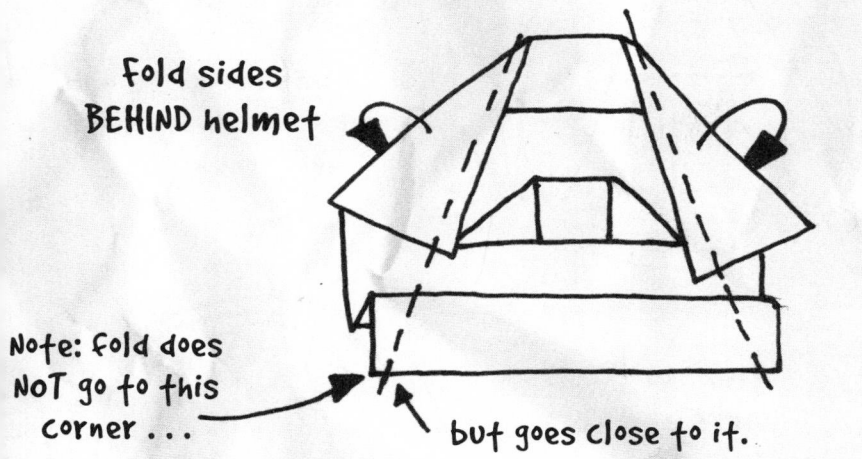

(9) Result . . .

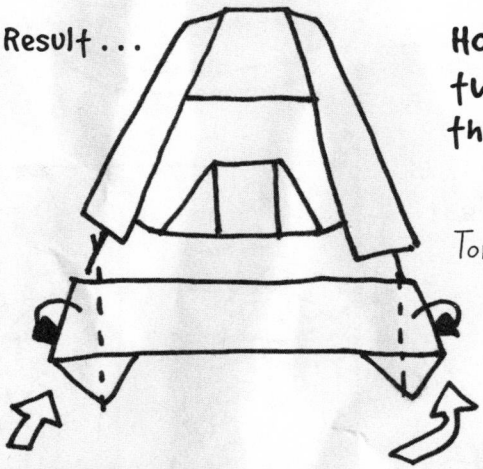

Hopefully, you will get two triangular legs at the bottom. If not, try re-doing step 8.

Tommy's note: Impossible!

Now fold the sides back—being careful NOT to fold helmet again, just the lower sides.

Result . . .

(10)

Now make Vader's famous helmet eyebrows.

Hold X with right thumb. Push paper upward with left thumb.

(11) Now switch fingers and push up the other side. Be careful not to rip it.

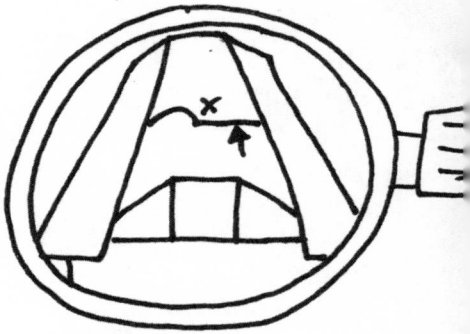

(12) Decorate and put a lightsaber in pleat.

To use . . .

Put finger in pleat. (or) Put finger under mask.

Tommy's comment: Don't get upset if it looks lame the first time. Even Harvey needed practice to get all those gaps and folds in the right places!

Everybody always asks me how to have Anakin's head under the mask . . . That's the genius part of MY version of Darth Paper. Anakin's head is already in there!

If you pull up on Darth Paper's mask, you'll think it won't come up. But if you pull on one side at a time . . . a hidden PLEAT will pop loose!

Pop both sides loose and you'll find the perfect spot to draw Anakin's face!

ORIGAMI YODA VS. DARTH PAPER

BY KELLEN

YOU CAN MAKE YOUR ORIGAMI PUPPETS FIGHT

FIRST ONE TO HIT THE GROUND IS THE LOSER!

TRY OTHER FAMOUS DUELS... LUKE VS. VADER, DARTH MAUL VS. OBI-WAN, PRINCIPAL RABBSKI VS. COMMON DECENCY!

KIRIGAMI GENERAL GRIEVOUS

BY DWIGHT AND KELLEN

KIRIGAMI LIKE ORIGAMI IS, BUT THE PAPER CUT WITH SCISSORS IS. OPEN UP MILLIONS OF NEW POSSIBILITIES IT DOES...

LAME!

IF YOU CUT THE PAPER, THEN IT'S NOT REAL ORIGAMI! JUST LAME ORIGAMI!

WHO DARES TO CALL ME LAME?

UH, NOT ME!

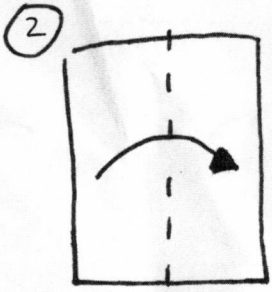

FOLD IN HALF.

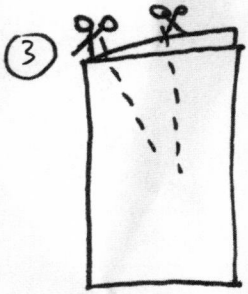

CUT THROUGH BOTH LAYERS.

UNFOLD.

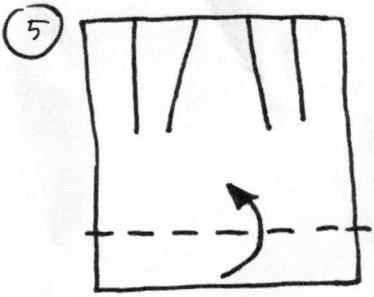

FOLD UP ABOUT 1/2 INCH.

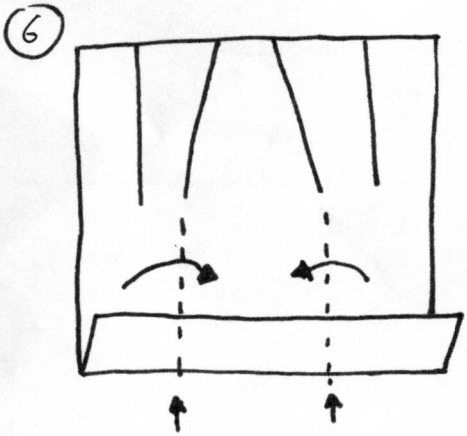

FOLD SIDES OVER.

NOTE THAT DOTTED LINES MATCH UP WITH BOTTOM OF THE INNER CUTS YOU MADE IN STEP 3.

6 1/2 IF YOU CAN, TUCK THE FLAPS TOGETHER, LIKE WITH BASIC PUPPET. IT'S HARDER HERE BECAUSE THEY'RE INSIDE!

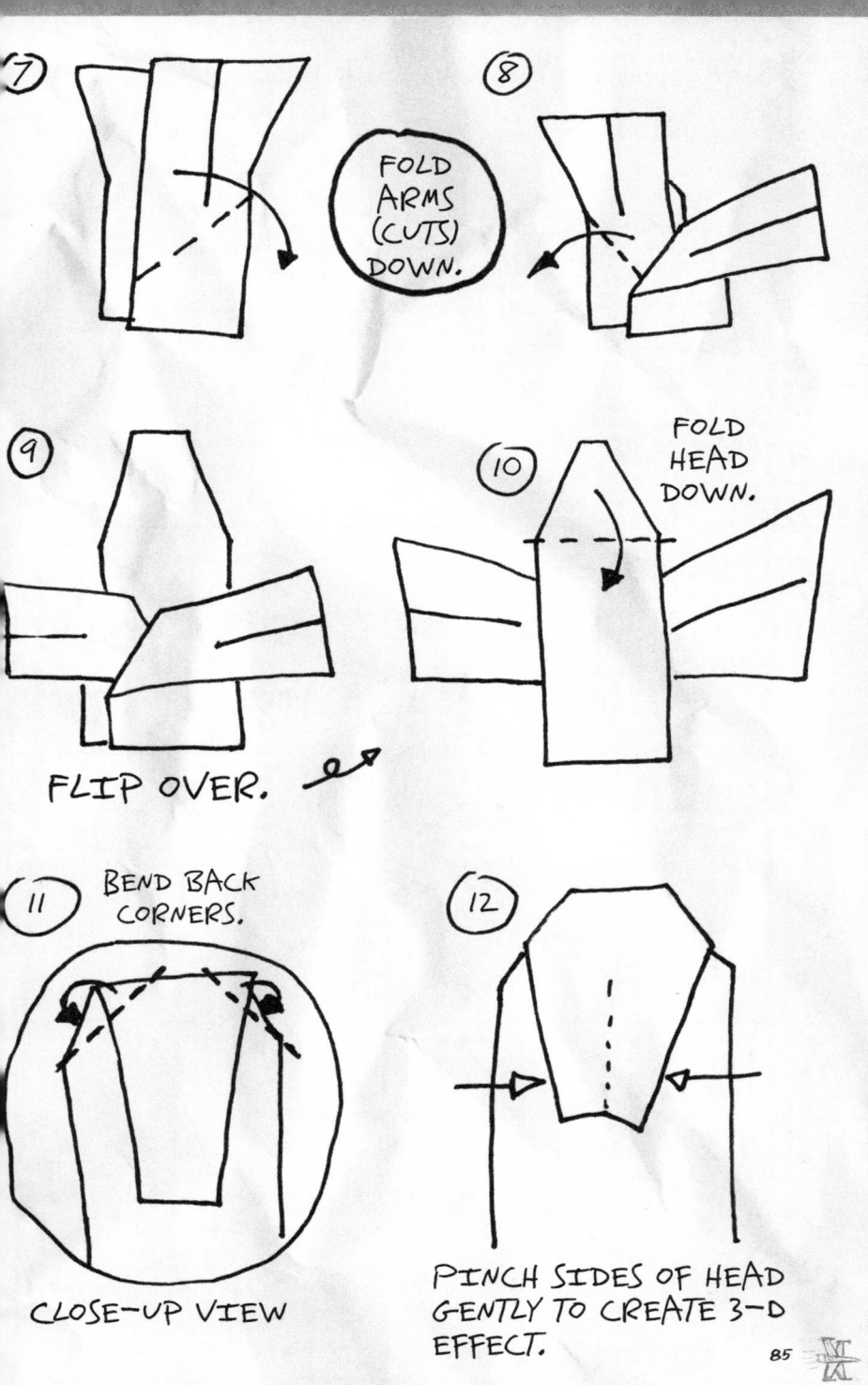
7
FOLD ARMS (CUTS) DOWN.
8
9
10
FOLD HEAD DOWN.
FLIP OVER.
11
BEND BACK CORNERS.
CLOSE-UP VIEW
12
PINCH SIDES OF HEAD GENTLY TO CREATE 3-D EFFECT.

13 SEPARATE, BEND, FOLD, AND SQUASH ARMS INTO SCARY, JEDI-HATING POSE!

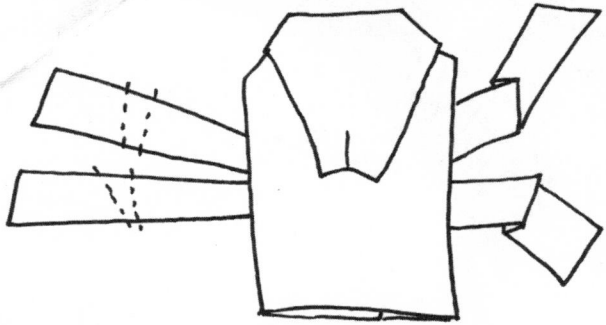

14

DRAW FACE.

15 ADD LIGHTSABERS OR OTHER USEFUL ITEMS.

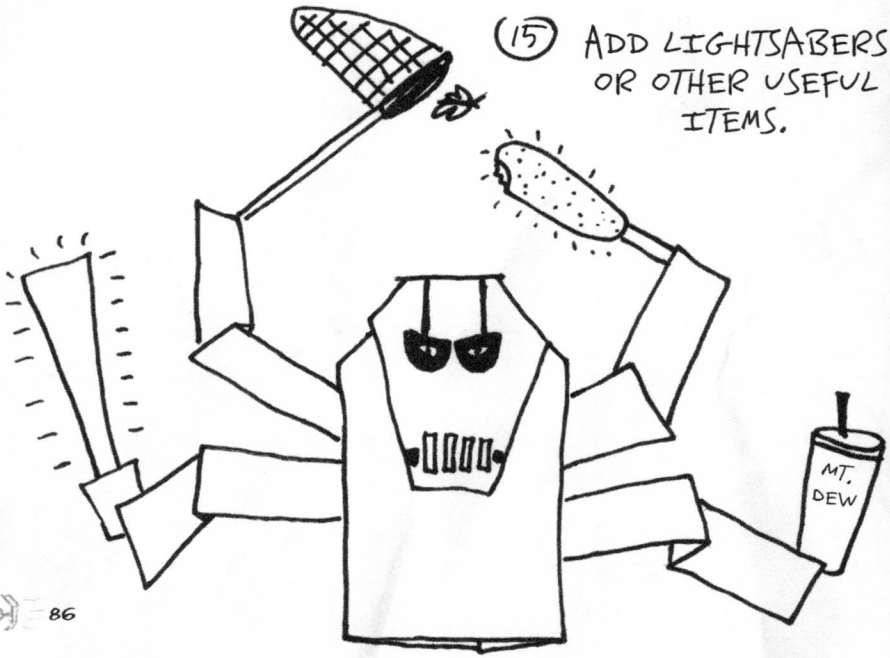

ORIGAMI COSTUMES

BY SARA, TOMMY, AND KELLEN

1. SEE IF YOU CAN TALK A TEACHER INTO GIVING YOU FOUR OR FIVE FEET OF BULLETIN BOARD PAPER. (THEY'VE PROBABLY GOT GIANT ROLLS OF IT HIDDEN IN THE TEACHERS' LOUNGE OR SOMEWHERE . . .)

2. IF NOT, YOU'LL HAVE TO FIND AN ART, PAPER, PARTY, OR CRAFTS STORE. ONCE YOU FIND THE PAPER, IT'S PRETTY CHEAP.

3. FOLD YOUR ORIGAMI. (YOU'LL WANT TO PRACTICE WITH A SMALL PIECE OF PAPER FIRST, OF COURSE.) FOR THE BIG ONE, USE PLENTY OF TAPE.

4. CHOOSE HOW YOU ARE GOING TO WEAR IT: OVER YOUR HEAD OR WITH A HOLE FOR YOUR HEAD. CUT EYEHOLES . . . OR . . . CUT A HEAD HOLE.

NOTE: DON'T CUT THE HOLES WHILE YOU ARE INSIDE!!! MURKY KNEW A KID WHO CUT OFF HIS NOSE THIS WAY AND HAS TO WEAR A FAKE ONE, NO JOKE!!!

FOLDING 1,000 YODAS

BY ORIGAMI MASTER BEN AND KELLEN

GET 250 SHEETS OF PAPER . . .

CUT THEM IN HALF . . .

CUT THOSE IN HALF . . .

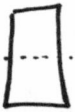

NOW YOU HAVE 1,000 RECTANGLES!

CHOOSE

FIVE-FOLD YODAS LIKE IN THE DARTH PAPER CASE FILE . . . A HUGE TASK

OR REGULAR YODAS FROM THE ORIGAMI YODA CASE FILE . . A MONSTER HUGE TASK!!!

EITHER WAY . . . MUCH PATIENCE WILL YOU NEED!

GAIN JEDI WISDOM YOU WILL?

OR JUST BIG MESS?

YOU CAN FIND INSTRUCTIONS FOR BOTH YODAS ON TOMMY'S WEB SITE: ORIGAMIYODA.COM

DON'T WASTE THE COLOR PAGES

BY KELLEN

PRACTICE ON REGULAR PAPER BEFORE YOU PULL OUT THESE COLOR PAGES TO USE FOR YOUR ORIGAMI!!!!! DO YOU KNOW HOW MUCH IT COST TO HAVE THEM PRINTED? A LOT!!!!!

WHEN WE FOUND OUT HOW MUCH, I HAD TO ASK MY MOM FOR THE EXTRA MONEY. SHE SAID SHE WOULD GIVE IT TO ME IF I WOULD LET HER PUT AN AD IN THE CASE FILE.

SHE SAID IT WOULD BE LIKE A PUBLIC SERVICE MESSAGE. I DIDN'T HAVE A CHOICE, SO HERE IT IS . . .

Kellen,

I am so proud of you and the other kids for putting this book together. Your drawings and projects are really wonderful, and you all have very promising futures . . .

. . . if you can learn how to do things more neatly.

I just can't understand why you would work so hard on something like this and then let it get all crumpled up.

And the handwriting! How can you expect other people to read your comics if you are going to scrawl the words in the speech balloons?

So keep it neat and you'll go far!

Love,

MOM!

Harvey's Comment

How embarrassing . . . especially since she's right!

FOLDING THE COLOR PAGES...

DWIGHT SAYS THE HARDEST THING ABOUT ORIGAMI CAN BE FINDING THE COLOR PAPER YOU WANT. HERE WE'VE GIVEN YOU COLOR COMBINATIONS FOR MAKING FIVE COOL STAR WARS CHARACTERS. SO, LIKE I SAID BEFORE, USE THIS PAPER CAREFULLY. FOLD ALONG THE PERFORATED LINE BEFORE YOU TEAR THE PAPER OUT AND MAYBE PRACTICE ON REGULAR PAPER FIRST.

- THE GRAY/WHITE SHEET IS FOR FOLDING ART2-D2. USE THE INSTRUCTIONS FROM PAGE 70. START WITH THE PAPER WHITE SIDE UP, SO THAT THE FIRST FOLD CREATES A GRAY DOME ON TOP OF A WHITE BODY.
- THE GOLD/GOLD PAPER IS FOR C-3PO. USE THE INSTRUCTIONS FROM PAGE 72.
- THE BROWN/GREEN PAPER IS FOR YODA. USE THE INSTRUCTIONS FROM PAGE 73. START WITH THE GREEN SIDE UP, SO THAT THE FIRST FOLD FORMS HIS BROWN ROBE. OR YOU CAN USE THE INSTRUCTIONS FROM TOMMY'S FIRST CASE FILE, THE STRANGE CASE OF ORIGAMI YODA. TO DO THAT ONE, START WITH THE BROWN SIDE UP. TOMMY HAS ALSO POSTED THOSE INSTRUCTIONS TO HIS WEB SITE, ORIGAMIYODA.COM.
- THE ORANGE/WHITE PAPER IS FOR ADMIRAL ACKBAR. USE THE INSTRUCTIONS FROM PAGE 74. START WITH THE ORANGE SIDE UP, SO THAT THE FIRST FOLD CREATES HIS WHITE UNIFORM.
- THE BLACK/BLACK PAPER IS FOR DARTH PAPER! YOU CAN USE THE (NEARLY IMPOSSIBLE) INSTRUCTIONS FOR HARVEY'S DARTH PAPER ON PAGE 76. OR YOU CAN USE BEN'S MUCH SIMPLER INSTRUCTIONS FROM TOMMY'S SECOND CASE FILE, DARTH PAPER STRIKES BACK, WHICH ARE ALSO ON ORIGAMIYODA.COM.

PHOTOGRAPHING DOODLE-GAMI PUPPETS

BY RHONDELLA

Uh . . . doodle-gami? You're actually calling it doodle-gami?

Only you guys could make *Star Wars* finger puppets MORE embarrassing!

Anyway, the only reason I'm doing this is because you all are always sending me these dark, blurry pictures of stuff. Like this . . .

Seriously? Even before I was on the yearbook staff I could take better pictures than that!

So, I'm going to give you some tips on taking better photos of your stuff.

Here's your Mandalinkian or whatever it's called. It looks about ten million times better, huh?

Well, here's how to do it . . .

Tip #1: BEWARE OF THE DARK SIDE!

You don't need a fancy camera or special lens or super-bright lights . . . you just need to . . .

GO OUTSIDE! Your pictures will instantly be a lot better if you just take them outside. During the DAY, obviously! The best thing you can do is to go out on a bright day, but find a place in the shade . . .

But make sure it's not a place that's got some shade AND some sun: that's distracting!

The one below was taken just a few inches away . . . where the sun wasn't hitting it directly . . .

Tip #2: FOCUS

See how the picture above is kinda blurry? I got too close!

If your camera has a "macro" or "flower" setting, use it!

If not, stay back and then zoom in using an app or online photo fixer. (There are plenty of free ones.)

Tip #3: SET UP A BACKDROP!

Don't be scared by the word "backdrop" . . . I just mean a blank piece of paper. This will help your origami stand out and also it will mean I don't have to see any more pictures of an origami dude standing on a wrinkly blanket.

Colored paper like construction paper works great.

Just put it down in a good place (tip #1) then put the origami down in the middle of it, then take your picture using tip #2.

This is all about getting rid of distractions so people get a good look at your origami and not my mom's sh'nasty old tablecloth! Here's me taking a picture of me taking a picture of that monkey pet of Jabba's.

It turned out pretty good . . .

Tip #4: CHOOSE BACKDROP COLOR WISELY

If you spend $1 to get a pack of different colored construction paper, you'll be able to pick the color that's right for each puppet . . .

Darth Maul kind of blends into the black one and you can't even see his horns on the white one. So pick a completely different color for him.

Now you can really see him!

You know what else would be cool? If you used a computer to make a really awesome backdrop.

Then you could just drop the origami on there and TA-DA!

I guess I must be the nicest girl in the whole school, because I made two for you. I downloaded the *Star Wars* logo at starwars.com.

STAR
WARS®

HOW TO DRAW...
PEOPLE
AND OTHERS

HOW TO DRAW SHIRTS AND PANTS

BY KELLEN

IT MIGHT SEEM LIKE PEOPLE ARE HARD TO DRAW . . . BECAUSE THEY ARE HARD TO DRAW. BUT IT ISN'T IMPOSSIBLE IF YOU TAKE IT ONE PIECE AT A TIME. STARTING WITH . . . A SHIRT, WHICH IS EASY.

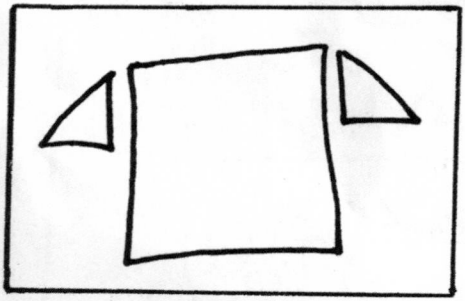

IT'S JUST TWO TRIANGLES STUCK ON THE SIDES OF A RECTANGLE . . .

WITH A "U" IN THE MIDDLE FOR THE NECK HOLE.

MAKE THE TRIANGLES A BIT CURVY, AND DON'T DRAW ALL THE LINES.

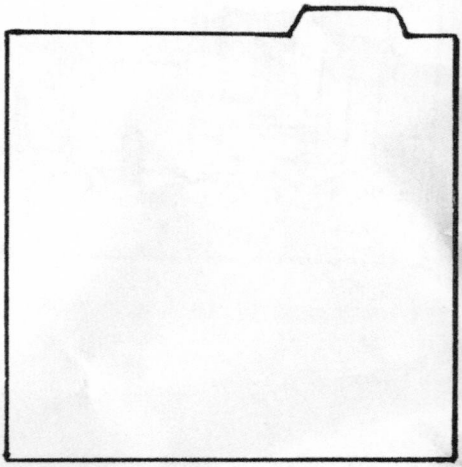

PRACTICE HERE UNTIL YOU HAVE MASTERED THE SHIRT.

NOW ADD SOME PANTS...

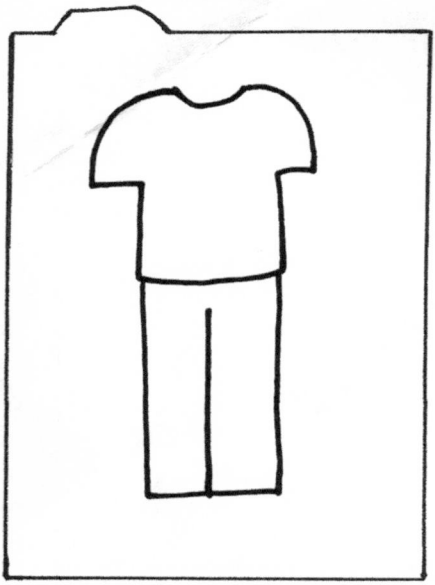

THEY'RE JUST A RECTANGLE WITH A LINE DOWN THE MIDDLE OR AN UPSIDE-DOWN "V"... AND SHORTS ARE JUST SHORT PANTS!

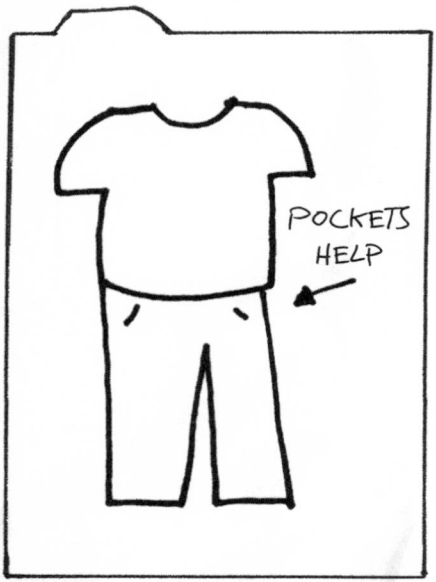

PRACTICE HERE UNTIL YOU HAVE MASTERED DRAWING SHIRTS AND PANTS TOGETHER . . .

HOW TO DRAW SHOES

BY KELLEN

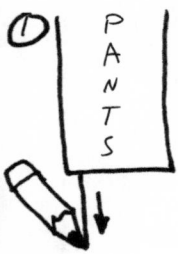

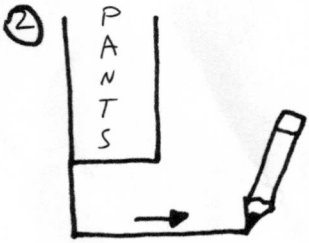

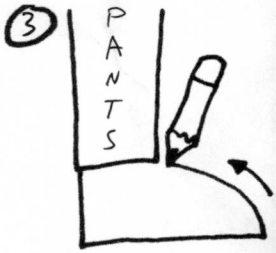

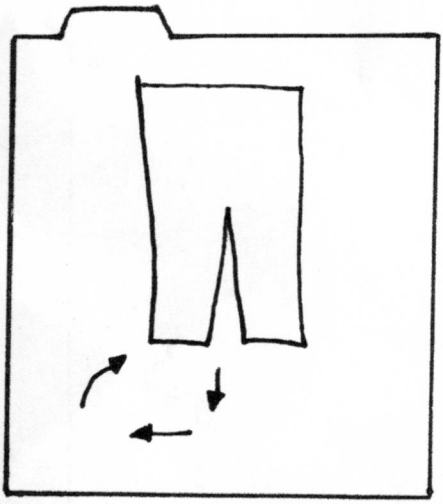

JUST CHANGE ONE OR MORE OF THOSE THREE LINES...

TO GET LOTS OF DIFFERENT SHOE SHAPES!

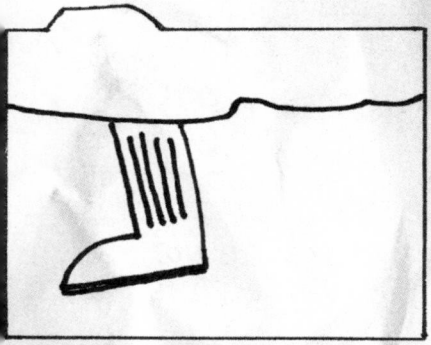

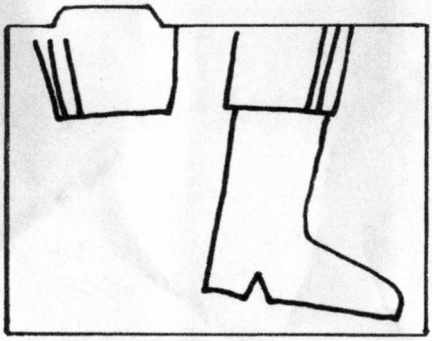

OR MAKE LINE 1 LONG ENOUGH TO MAKE LEIA'S AND HAN'S BOOTS.

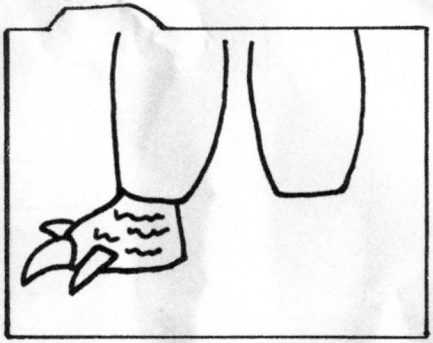

ADD SOME CLAWS FOR BOSSK.

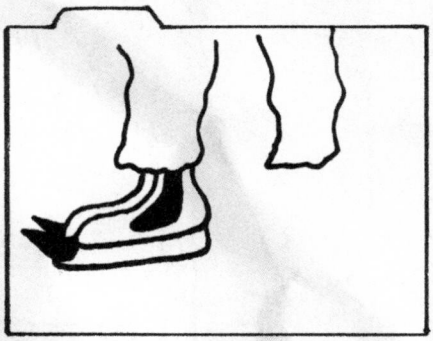

DON'T FORGET BOBA'S TOE SPIKES!

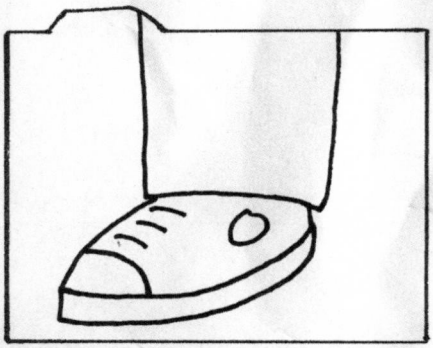

CURVE LINE 2 TO GIVE 3-D EFFECT.

BONUS TIP: DON'T FORGET STINK LINES FOR HARVEY'S SHOES!

HOW TO DRAW FAKE HANDS & ARMS

BY KELLEN

HANDS AND ARMS ARE HARD!!! IF YOU'RE NOT IN THE MOOD FOR A STRUGGLE, JUST TRY THESE FAKE ONES...

DRAW LINE DOWN BESIDE SHIRT...

DRAW MY OTHER ARM, PLEASE

ADD A CURVE FOR THE HAND AND EITHER A "U" OR A BACKWARD "J" FOR THE THUMB.

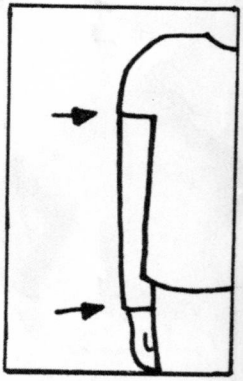

FOR LONG SLEEVES, JUST MOVE LINE DOWN.

A QUICK NOTE ABOUT WRITING ON T-SHIRTS:

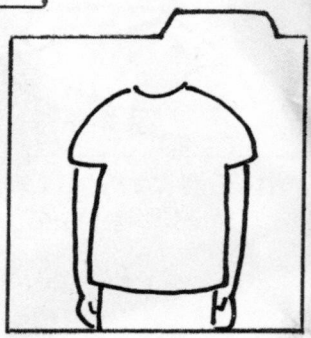

SHOW ME YOUR MASTERY OF FAKE HANDS AND ARMS . . .

HOW TO DRAW HEADS

BY KELLEN

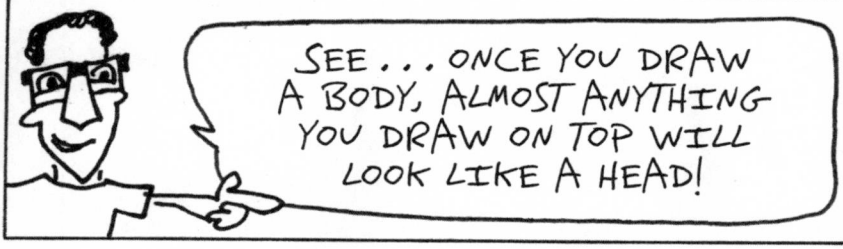

TRY IT OUT . . . DON'T WORRY ABOUT THE FACES YET. A SMILEY WILL DO.

HOW TO DRAW EYES

BY KELLEN

FIRST OF ALL... DON'T DRAW EYES LIKE THIS!

IT'S JUST GOING TO MAKE PEOPLE LOOK ALL FREAKY! UNLESS IT'S AHSOKA.

EYES COME IN LOTS OF SHAPES, SO YOU REALLY NEED TO LOOK AT A PERSON BEFORE YOU DRAW THEIR EYES!

ME (KELLEN)

TOMMY

REMI

HARVEY

GENERAL GRIEVOUS

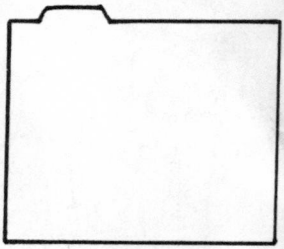

YOURS

ACTUALLY, SOME PEOPLE DO HAVE THE SAME SHAPE.

LOOK AT DIFFERENT PEOPLE AND TRY DRAWING JUST THEIR EYES . . .

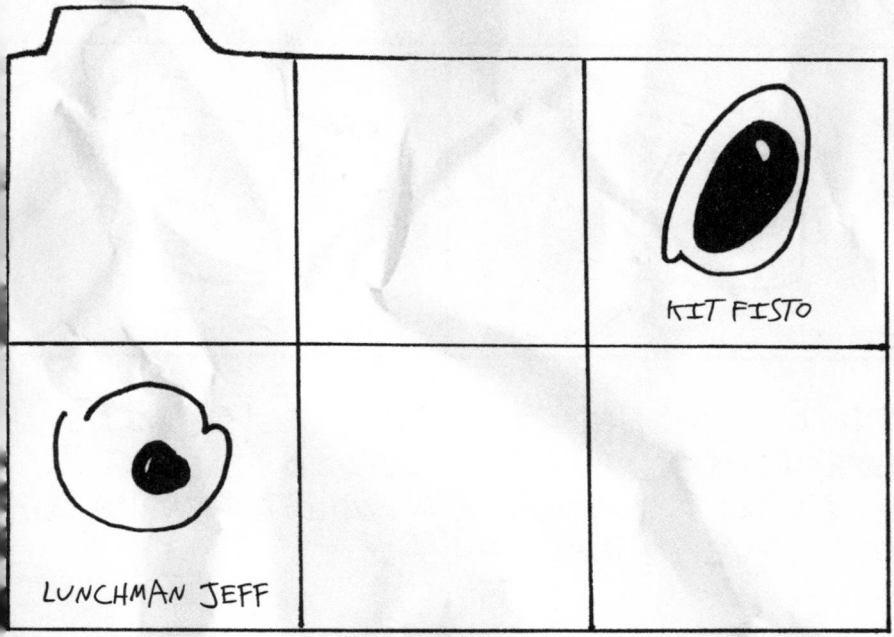

NOW TRY DRAWING THOSE SAME EYES TINY!

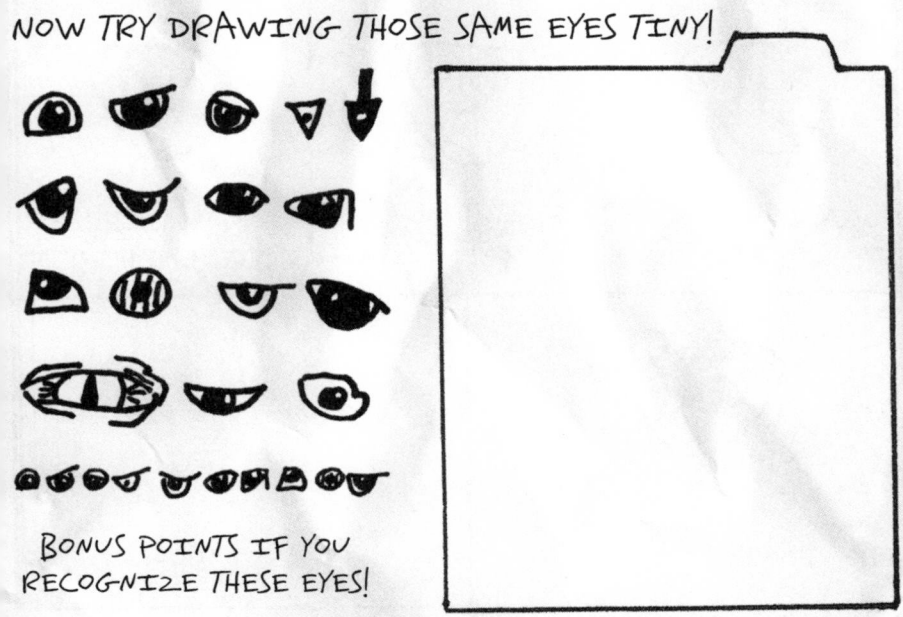

BONUS POINTS IF YOU RECOGNIZE THESE EYES!

WHAT'S THE DIFFERENCE BETWEEN THESE TWO PICTURES OF DWIGHT?

THE ONE ON THE RIGHT HAS "EYESHINE"! EYESHINE IS ALWAYS A GOOD IDEA... BUT UNLESS YOU HAVE A WHITE PEN HANDY, YOU HAVE TO PLAN AHEAD!

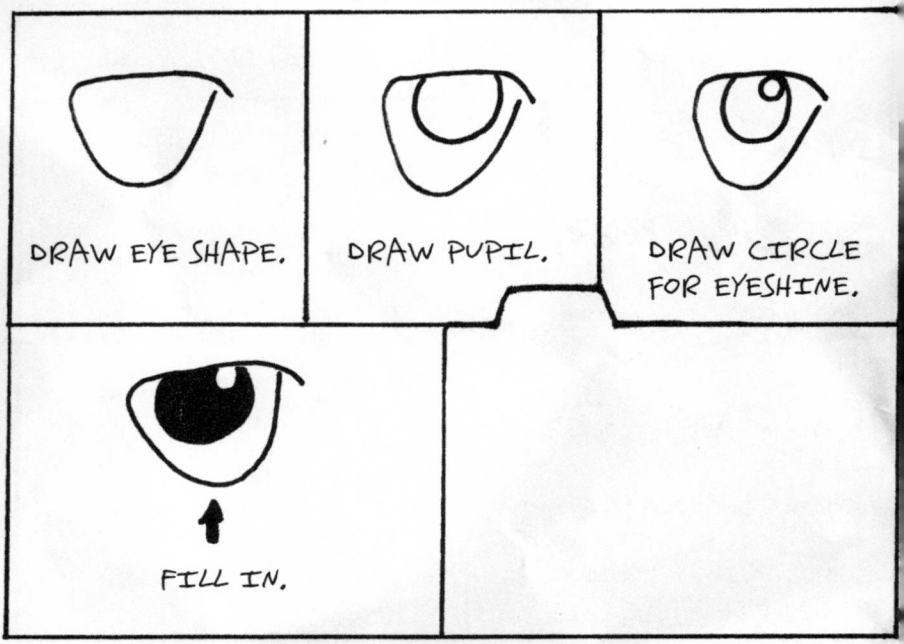

A WORD ABOUT GLASSES...

THEY CAN BE **HARD!!!**

I LIKE TO DRAW THE GLASSES FIRST AND THEN ADD THE EYES. HERE'S HOW TO DRAW HARVEY'S EYES AND GLASSES.

HOW TO DRAW FACES

BY KELLEN

ONCE YOU CAN DRAW EYES...

...A FACE IS JUST PUTTING A NOSE IN BETWEEN AND A LINE UNDERNEATH FOR A MOUTH.
(I LIKE TO ADD AN EXTRA LINE UNDER THE MOUTH LINE.)

THEN ADD SOME HAIR. AND DRAW A SINGLE LINE THAT STARTS WITH ONE EAR, GOES AROUND THE FACE, AND ENDS WITH THE OTHER EAR.

SARA

TRY THESE FACES . . .

TOMMY

LUNCHMAN JEFF

DRAW YOUR FAVORITE STAR WARS GOOD GUY.

DRAW YOUR FAVORITE STAR WARS BAD GUY.

DRAW YOURSELF AND YOUR BEST FRIEND . . .

HOW TO DRAW HANDS

BY KELLEN

HANDS ARE THE HARDEST THING IN THE UNIVERSE TO DRAW! I'M NOT CLAIMING TO BE ANY GOOD AT IT. (SO DON'T START, HARVEY!!!) BUT HERE ARE MY HAND-DRAWING SURVIVAL TIPS!

I TOOK A PICTURE OF TOMMY'S HAND, THEN LOADED IT UP ON MY COMPUTER. THEN I DREW A LINE AROUND IT. HERE'S WHAT I FOUND OUT...

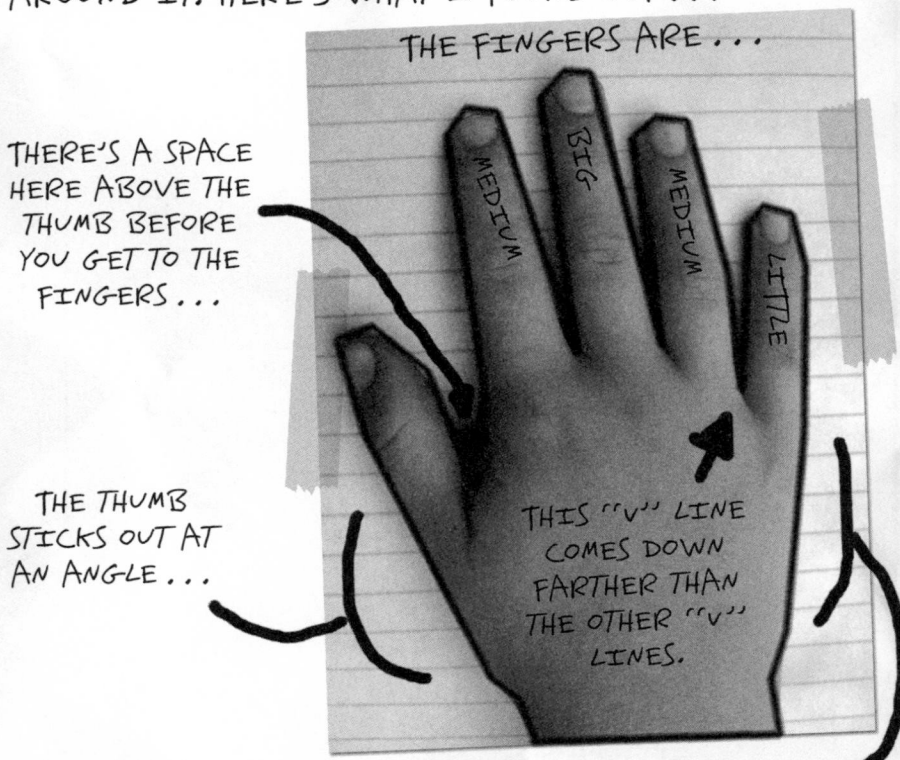

NOW LET'S SEE IF WE CAN USE ALL THAT INFO TO DRAW A HAND.

DRAWING A CLOSED HAND IS A BIT EASIER

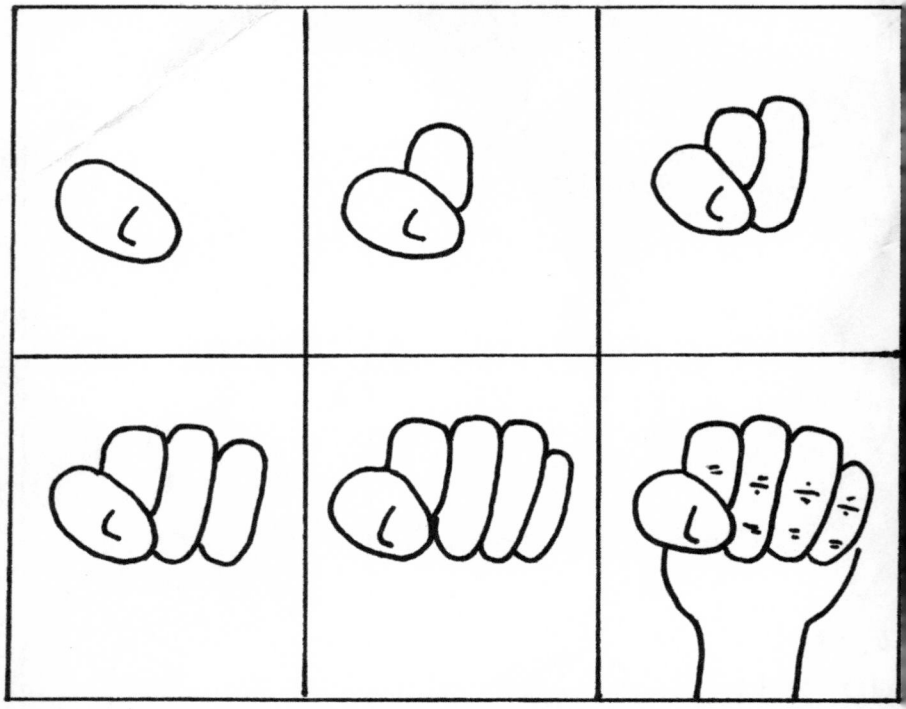

TRY A RIGHT HAND . . .

AND A LEFT . . .

THE BEST THING TO DO IS TO AVOID DRAWING HANDS IN THE FIRST PLACE! HAVE YOUR DOODLE PERSON HOLD A:

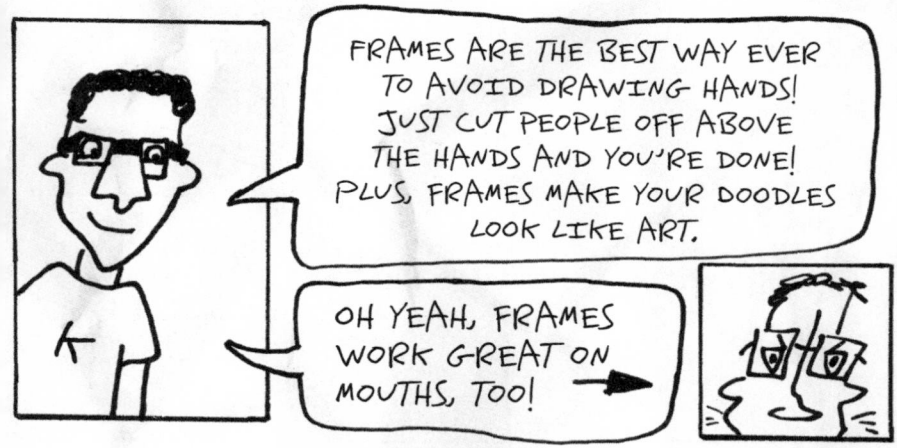

...AND THEN DRAW ANOTHER LINE NEXT TO IT... AND ADD A HAND.

AND I BET YOU'RE GOING TO SAY THE SAME THING ABOUT LEGS, TOO?
UH... YES?
I ♥ JOGGING!
DRAW OUTSIDES OF LEGS.
THEN INSIDES.
THEN SHOES!
SO BASICALLY... YOU'RE OKAY WITH STICK FIGURES AS LONG AS THEY HAVE A FEW EXTRA STICKS?
YES!
GIVE BOBA FETT LEGS...

NOW THAT YOU'VE MASTERED PEOPLE, IT'S TIME FOR . . .

ACTUAL BOOKMARK

HANDED OUT BY MR. GOOD CLEAN FUN
CONTRIBUTED BY TOMMY

HOW TO BLOW YOUR NOSE!

THIS BOOKMARK COULD SAVE YOUR LIFE!!!!!!!!!!!

Mr. Good Clean Fun and Soapy here to remind you of our five easy LIFE-SAVING steps for blowing your nose!

1) Wash hands before dispensing tissue from box.
2) Dispense the amount of tissues you need — DON'T BE WASTEFUL!!!
3) Completely cover nostrils and blow firmly, but politely.
4) After using your tissue, please dispose of it in a proper receptacle.
5) Wash hands — AGAIN — after using the tissue.

Follow these steps for fewer sick days and more GOOD CLEAN FUN Days!

Photocopy this page and cut out your own bookmark.

HOW TO TALK LIKE YODA

BY HARVEY

okay . . . now I'm going to add something USEFUL to this case file! I think the one thing we can all agree on is that I do the best Yoda impression around here!

The important thing is to know what order to put the words in.

It is NOT just saying them backward! That's a common mistake, but WRONG!

WRONG!

I talk like Yoda!

Yoda like talk I!

See? That stinks! And you can't fix it just by adding "do" to the end . . . like SOME people do.

Yoda like talk I do!

Instead, you need to move the subject to the end . . .

① Talk like Yoda

Now is the time to add "do" or another verb to help the sentence make sense . . .

Talk like Yoda I do!

Now add a "hmmm" or a "yes?" . . .

Talk like Yoda I do, yes?

Sometimes it's better to move the subject AND the verb to the end . . .

Harvey is the greatest!

The greatest Harvey is!

Try these:
The dark side is powerful.
You must buy Cheetos for everyone.
Fools rush in.
Do you judge me by my size?

TRENCH RUN

THE 56¢ STAR WARS GAME

BY MIKE AND KELLEN

YOU WILL NEED: 25¢ 25¢ 1¢ 5¢

PLUS TWO PLAYERS, A TABLE, AND TWO OR MORE BOOKS!

FIRST . . . LEARN TO FIRE A PHOTON PENNY!

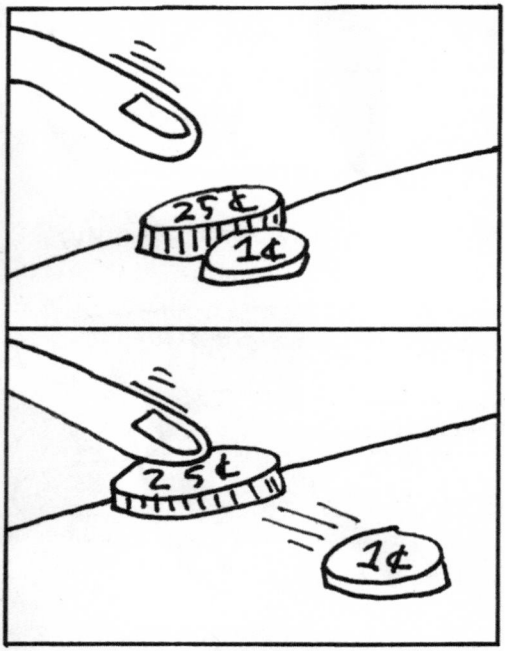

PLACE PENNY SO IT TOUCHES EDGE OF QUARTER.

THEN . . .

STRIKE QUARTER WITH ONE FINGER!

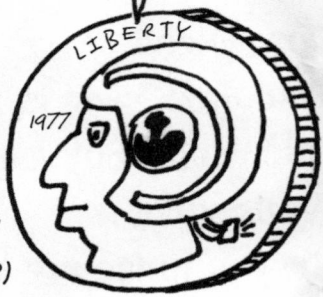

THE PENNY SHOOTS OFF!

(GEORGE WASHINGTON, REBEL LEADER)

SETUP

25¢

1¢

SISTERS GRIMM

DIARY OF A WIMPY KID

TARGET

25¢

QUARTER ON TOP OF NICKEL!

TABLE EDGE

RULES:

- TAKE TURNS FIRING PHOTON PENNIES.
- KNOCK NICKEL COMPLETELY CLEAR OF QUARTER TO GET POINT. = 1 25 = 5¢
- TOUCH BOOKS OR GO OFF TABLE AND YOU LOSE A TURN!
- TOO EASY? ADD MORE BOOKS! SLIDE BOOKS CLOSER TOGETHER! STACK EXTRA QUARTER ON TARGET!
- USE THE FORCE!

HOW TO MAKE A LIP BALM ROCKET

BY DWIGHT AND KELLEN

OPEN UP A TUBE OF LIP STUFF AND TURN THE KNOB TO CRANK THE LIP BALM ALL THE WAY OUT...

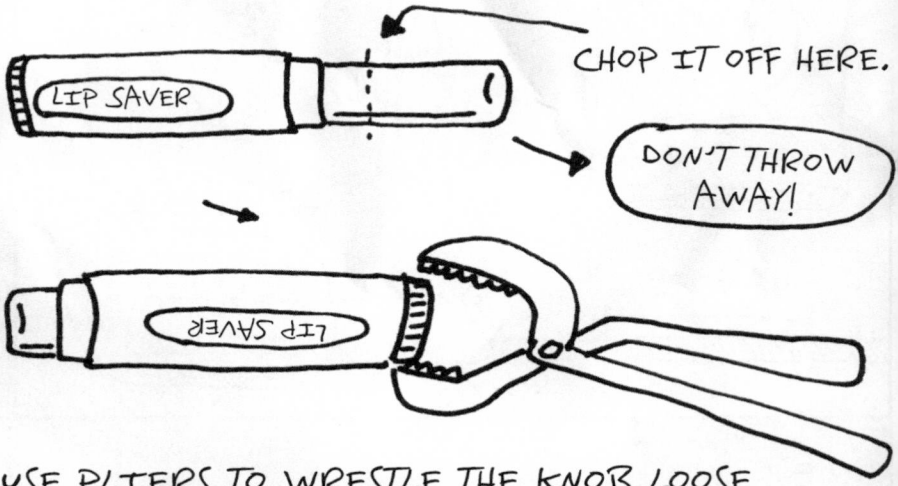

USE PLIERS TO WRESTLE THE KNOB LOOSE AT THE BOTTOM. (DO NOT USE A KNIFE!)

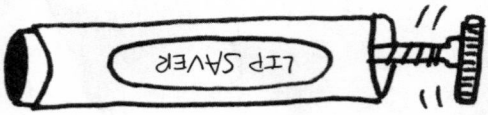

HOPEFULLY, KNOB WILL COME LOOSE BUT WILL STILL B CONNECTED TO SOMETHING INSIDE THE TUBE. IF NOT, CAN PROBABLY BE SCREWED BACK IN.

NOTE: DWIGHT'S METHOD OF BEATING ON THE TUBE WITH A VOLUME OF THE ENCYCLOPEDIA IS <u>NOT</u> RECOMMENDED! IT TAKES <u>FOREVER</u>!

NOW USE THE ACTUAL BALM STUFF TO GREASE THE MOUTH OF THE TUBE A LITTLE BIT. YOU MAY NEED TO APPLY MORE OR WIPE SOME OFF, DEPENDING ON HOW THINGS GO . . .

NOW PUT ON THE CAP . . .

WHEN THE PLUNGER GOES IN . . . THE CAP SHOULD POP OFF AND GO A LONG WAY!

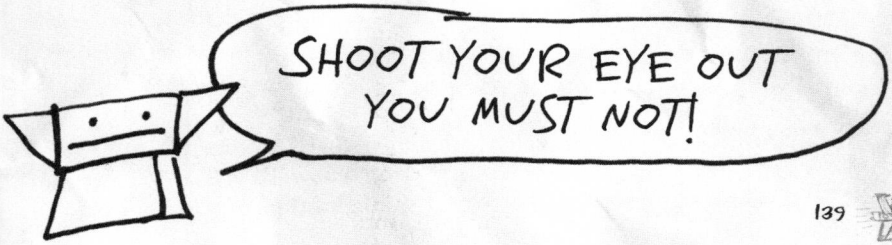

HOW DWIGHT FAKE-CRACKS HIS KNUCKLES

BY TOMMY

At last I have solved the mystery of how Dwight drives everyone crazy by fake-cracking his knuckles. Now I can do it, too! Here's how:

1. Put the index finger of your left hand between the index and middle fingers of your right hand.

2. It should look like this. The tip of your index finger is pushing down on the web between the other two fingers.

3. Now place all three fingers firmly against your chin. You must create an airtight seal so that a little pocket of air is formed above your left index finger.

4. Now bend your left index finger down quickly! When it pops loose from the other fingers, the air bubble should pop, too, making a loud CRACK!

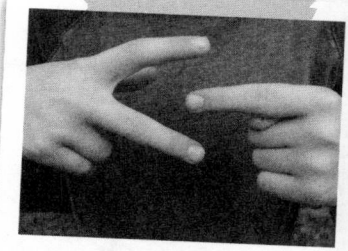

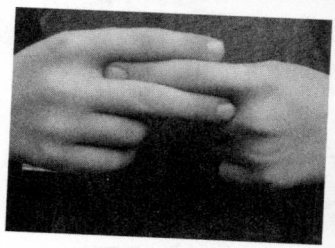

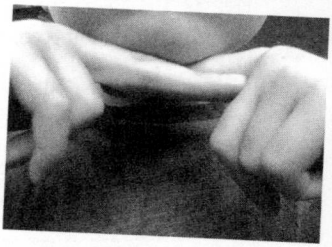

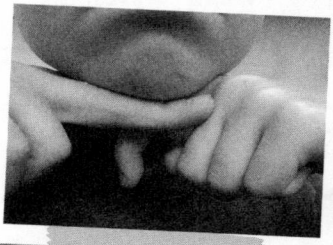

It takes a lot of practice, but soon you will be able to annoy a whole roomful of people!!! Good luck, and use your powers wisely!

HOW TO MAKE ERASER PRINTS

BY MURKY AND KELLEN

OKAY, YOU ARE GOING TO NEED ONE OF THOSE BIG ERASERS. SOME OF THEM ARE PINK. IT DOESN'T MATTER WHAT COLOR IT IS. I'M JUST SAYING THAT A LOT OF THEM ARE PINK.

YOU ALSO NEED A COUPLE OF DECENT MAGIC MARKERS BUT NOT SHARPIES. SHARPIES ARE STOOKY BUT NOT FOR THIS. YOU JUST NEED REGULAR DECENT MAGIC MARKERS FOR THIS.

SO DRAW A BUNCH OF HAIR ON THE FLAT PART OF THE ERASER. IT'S JUST A LOT OF LITTLE LINES SO DON'T WASTE A WHOLE LOT OF TIME. IF YOU DO, THE INK WILL DRY AND YOU'LL BE LIKE "HUH?"

AS SOON AS YOU FINISH DRAWING, FLIP IT OVER ON A PIECE OF PAPER AND SMOOSH IT DOWN MEGA HARD, THEN LIFT IT UP CAREFULLY SO YOU DON'T SMEAR IT.

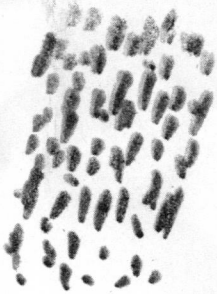

OKAY, NOW YOU SHOULD HAVE A PRINT LIKE THIS. IF YOU SMUDGE IT, DON'T WORRY. CHEWIE WON'T MIND.

NOW USE THE BLACK MARKER TO DRAW CHEWIE'S FACE ON THE ERASER.

AND DRAW THE BANDOLIER BACKWARDS.

YOU'RE MAKING A PRINT AND PRINTED STUFF COMES OUT BACKWARDS, SO DRAW IT BACKWARDS NOW OR IT WILL BE BACKWARDS LATER. AND DON'T WASTE TIME. DO IT QUICK.

NOW FLIP IT OVER ON TOP OF THE CHEWIE HAIR PRINT AND SMOOSH AGAIN.

YOU SHOULD GET SOMETHING LIKE THIS. IF NOT, JUST TRY AGAIN. THE ERASER WILL BE DRY IN TWO SECONDS.

TO MAKE CHEWIE'S ARMS

YOU CAN MAKE LOTS OF STAR WARS PEOPLE . . . EVEN ART2-D2!

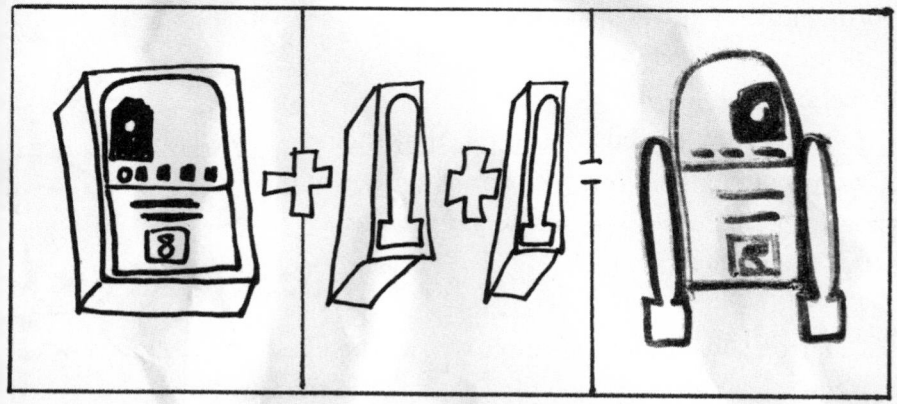

ACTION FIGURE AND SPACESHIP PRINTS

BY AMY

Okay, so this is not really doodling. You may end up with a big inky mess. Or you may end up with something good enough to hang in a museum. It's all a bit random, so just have fun!

You will need:

- Silly Putty (You can try stuff like modeling clay, but Silly Putty works great! I used three eggs' worth on the *Millennium Falcon*.)
- Stamp pad (You can also try using Magic Markers.)
- *Star Wars* toys! (If you are careful, they should be okay, but don't try this with a rare antique or something. And you'll see that some toys work better than others . . .)

1. Flatten Silly Putty into a blob the same size as the toy . . .

2. Then push the toy facedown into the Silly Putty . . .

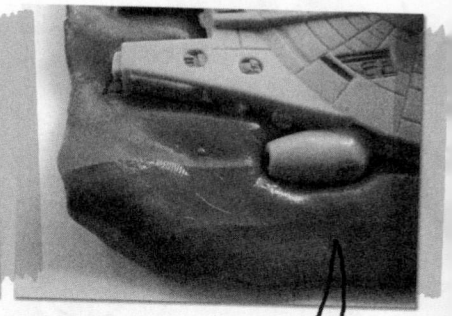

SIR . . . I'VE CALCULATED THAT THE ODDS OF SURVIVING A SILLY PUTTY ATTACK ARE . . .

NEVER TELL ME THE ODDS!

3. Carefully peel the putty off the toy . . . You now have a mold of the toy!

4. Working quickly, dab your finger on the ink pad, then dab it on the putty. Continue until the entire surface is good and inky! *Don't* try to fill in all the little nooks and crannies . . . those are what make the print!

5. Now flip the putty over so it is ink side down on the paper . . . and smoosh it all down really, really good with your fingers . . .

6. Now peel back the putty to reveal your print!!!

   Don't worry if it's not perfect . . . it's not supposed to be!

Tips:

- Just knead the putty a bit and you'll be ready to use it again!
- Which is good, because sometimes it takes three or four tries to get a good one.
- Try scanning or photographing your prints and adjusting the colors, contrast, and size.
- You can use two toys to make one print. For the Chewie print below, I molded a section of the Falcon, then I molded Chewie on top of that.
- Experimenting is key! Some figures, like Jabba, work great; some, like Salacious Crumb, don't (Crumb's nose is too pointy!).

Make a print here . . .

PENCIL PODRACING

BY MIKE

Okay, remember when Mr. Snider taught us how to play that old Pencil Wars game where X-wings and TIE fighters battle around the Death Star? Well, that game is stooky, but I actually like Pencil Podracing even better. We made it up, and here are the rules . . .

Just like with the other game, you move your ship/podracer with pencil flicks . . .

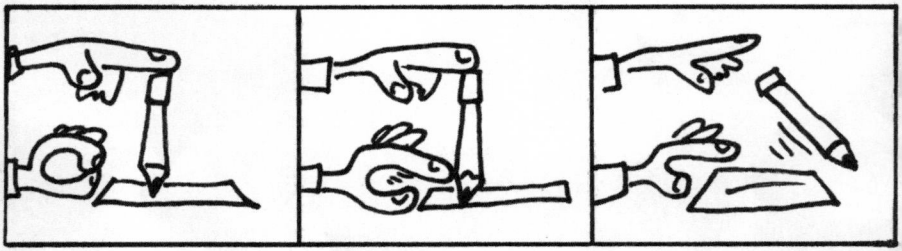

Press down on the eraser end of the pencil with your left index finger so that the tip is right in front of your podracer. Then flick the pencil near the bottom with your right index finger. If you do it right, it should make a mark on the paper . . . Wherever the mark goes, that's where your podracer goes! So redraw the podracer at the end of the mark.

In this game you race around an obstacle course. (Making the obstacle courses is almost as much fun as playing!) You have to flick the pencil so that you go as far as possible . . . but you also have to avoid all the obstacles!

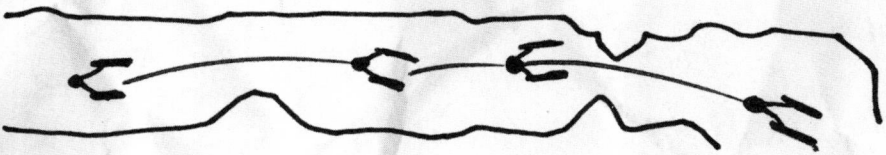

If you don't hit anything, you redraw your podracer at the end of the mark, and then the next person goes.
If you hit a wall, you redraw your podracer at the spot where you hit the wall, and your turn is over.
If you hit an obstacle with a label (such as -1 or -2), then your turn is over, and you also miss future turns . . .

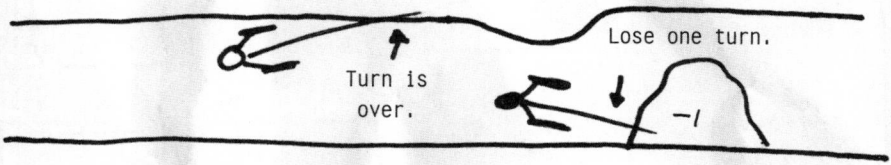

If you hit another podracer, they lose a turn! So playing like Sebulba can really pay off!

You may also hit something that gives you an extra turn (+1) or maybe a bunch of extra turns. But don't put in too many of these or the game gets dumb.

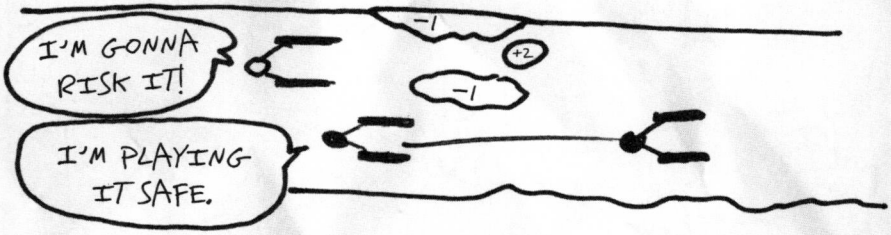

A well-designed course tempts the players into taking Anakin-level risks to get any rewards!

Beginner podracing course

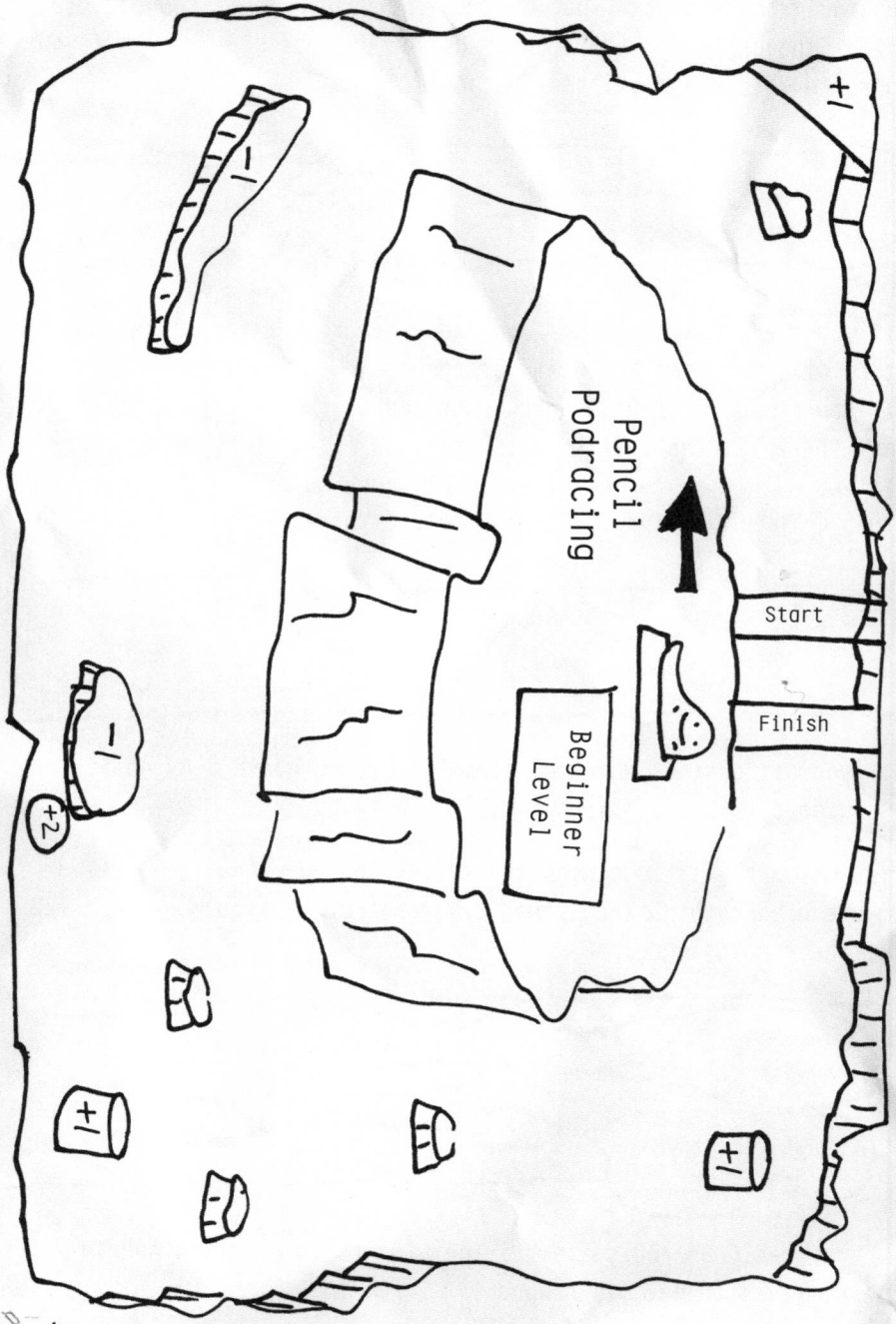

Draw your own . . .

Expert podracing course

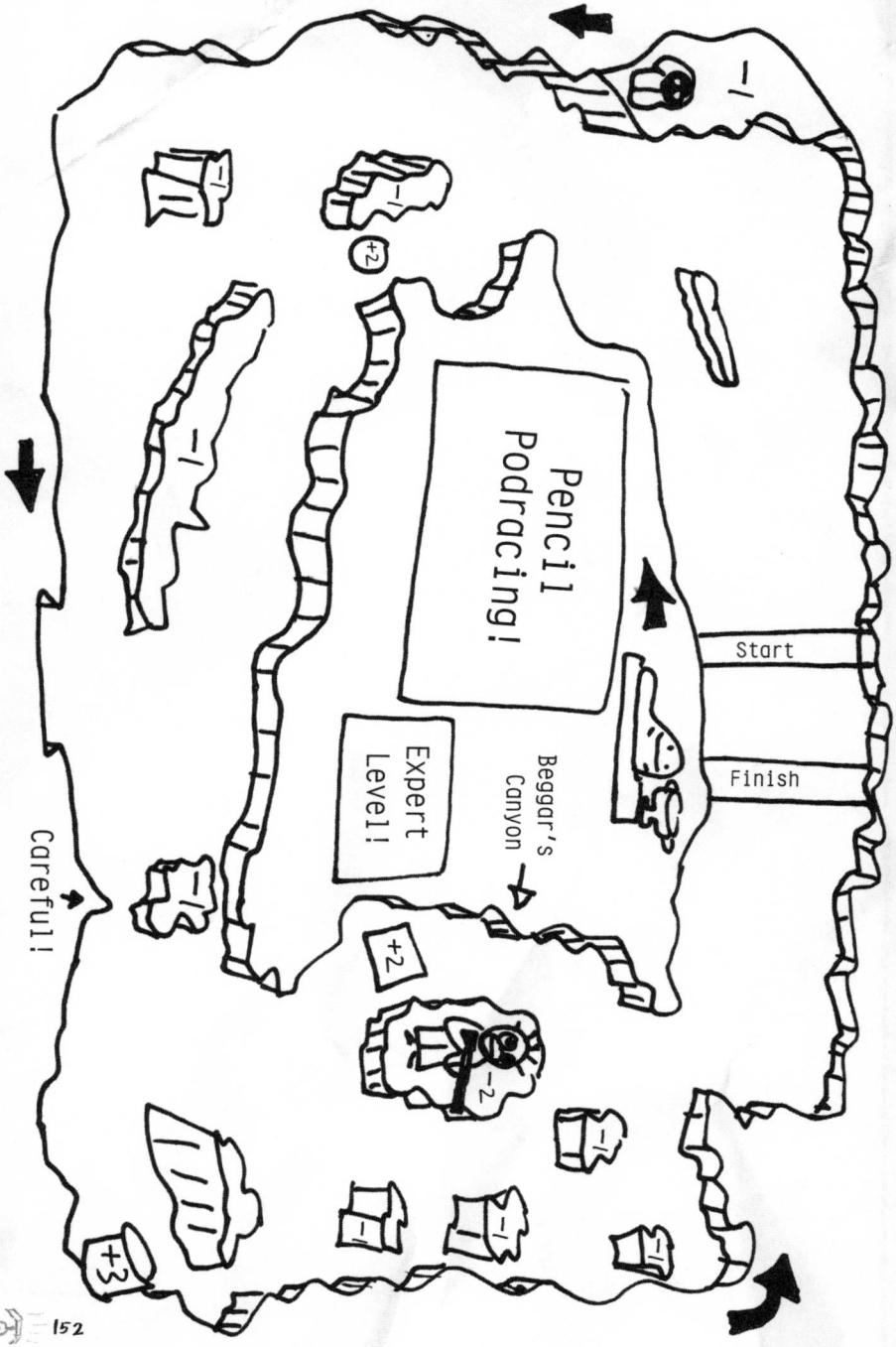

Draw your own . . .

HOW TO MAKE YOUR OWN ORIGAMI YODA T-SHIRT

BY KELLEN

WARNING: THIS PROJECT IS A GREAT WAY TO MAKE YOUR MOM MAD! I KNOW THAT FOR A FACT! SO USE SOME COMMON SENSE . . . MAKE IT OUTSIDE, USE AN OLD SHIRT, BE CAREFUL WITH THE SPRAY PAINT, ETC. . . .

YOU WILL NEED:

- WHITE T-SHIRT
- GREEN SPRAY PAINT
- SCISSORS
- TAPE
- BLACK SHARPIE
- SCRAP PAPER
- FLAT SPOT OUTSIDE
- A BUNCH OF PENNIES (AND MAYBE A DIME)

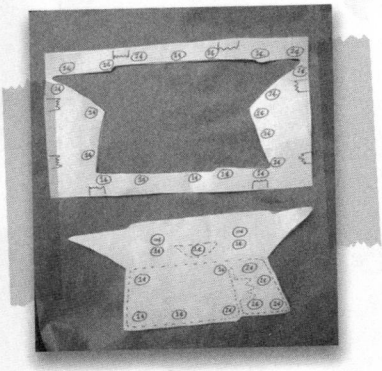

1. CUT OUT STENCIL PAGE AND CUT OUT STENCIL ON SOLID BLACK OUTLINE.

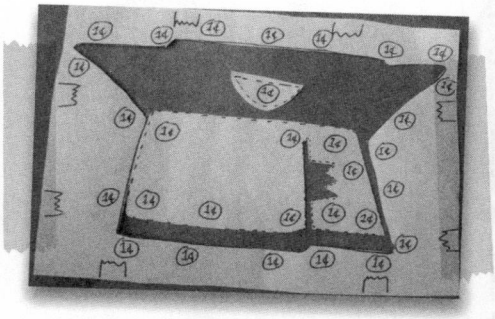

2. CUT OUT THE INSIDE PIECES OF THE STENCIL.

3. NOW LAY THE SHIRT ON SOMETHING FLAT THAT YOU WON'T GET IN TROUBLE IF YOU GET PAINT ON IT. I USED THE LID OF A PLASTIC TUB . . .

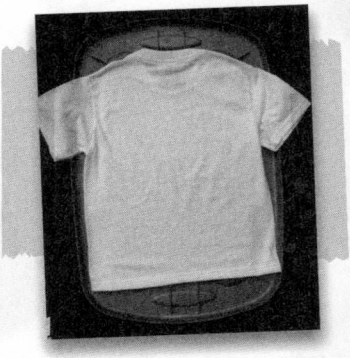

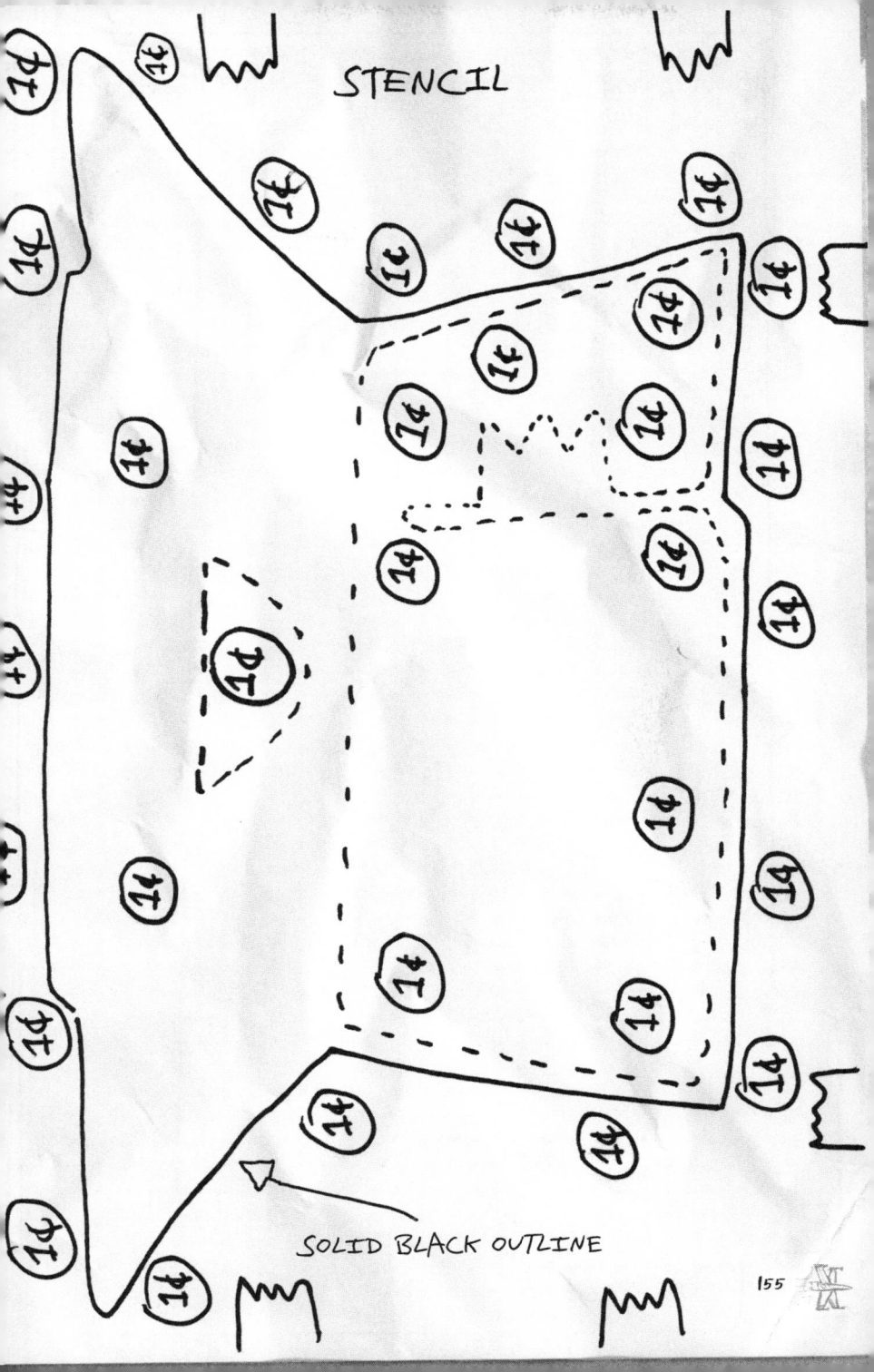
STENCIL
SOLID BLACK OUTLINE

IF YOU'RE NOT GOING TO MAKE A T-SHIRT, YOU MAY AS WELL DOODLE HERE. BUT IF YOU ARE GOING TO, THEN DON'T DOODLE HERE, BECAUSE YOU'LL HAVE TO CUT IT UP!

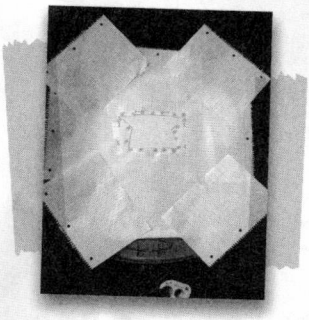

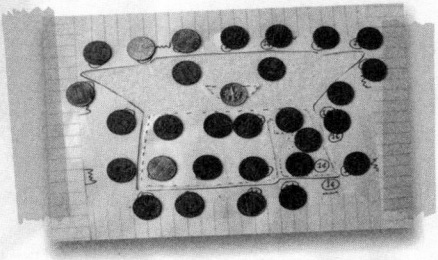

4. LAY STENCIL IN THE CENTER OF THE T-SHIRT (TWO OR THREE INCHES BELOW THE NECK HOLE). TAPE SCRAP PAPER TO THE EDGES OF THE STENCIL AND ALL AROUND. COVER AS MUCH OF THE SHIRT AS POSSIBLE.

5. NOW USE THE PENNIES TO ANCHOR THE STENCIL IN PLACE, LEAVING T-SHIRT EXPOSED. YOU MAY NEED TO USE A DIME ON THE MOUTH, IF IT'S TOO SMALL. AND ADD TWO EXTRA PENNIES TO CREATE THE EYES!!!!

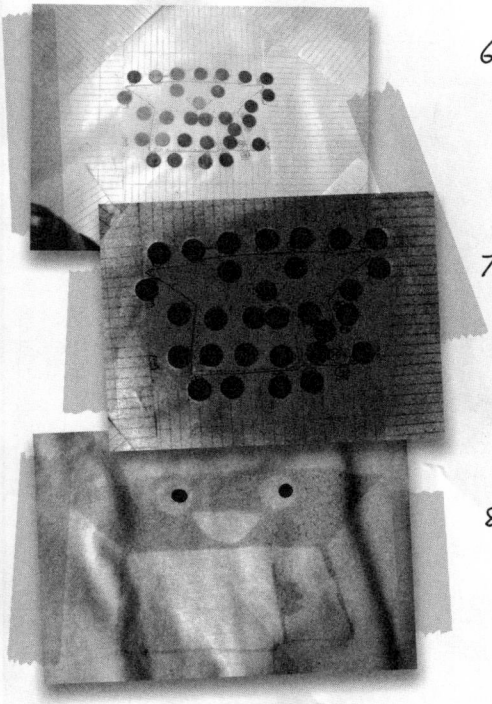

6. START SPRAYING! DON'T GET TOO CLOSE . . . IF YOU BLAST THE STENCIL, THE PAINT WILL GET UNDERNEATH IT!

7. GIVE IT A FEW MINUTES TO DRY. THEN CAREFULLY PEEL EVERYTHING OFF AND YOU SHOULD SEE ORIGAMI YODA UNDERNEATH!

8. ADD EYES WITH A SHARPIE AND WEAR YOUR SHIRT WITH PRIDE!!!!!!! (LOOKS BETTER IN COLOR.)

Great, what am I supposed to do with a bunch of green pennies? ← Harvey's Comment

THE END IS THE BEGINNING

BY TOMMY

Well, I have to admit I was a little disappointed at first. Not really with the case file but with my doodling and stuff.

My AT-AT looks like Luke has already blown it up. My lip balm rocket hit my brother in the head, and I got in huge trouble. My T-shirt turned out okay, but I wish I had used green paint, because everybody who sees it asks me, "Uh, why is Yoda red? Is it, like, Darth Yoda or something?" And also, yes, I managed to make my mom mad by getting paint on the driveway.

But my doodling is the worst! All my pictures of people look like I'm trying to insult them.

About the only thing I got right was a perfect picture of an Ugnaught. Unfortunately, I was TRYING to draw Sara when I made it! And as far as drawing hands . . . forget it!

So I felt like a total loser . . . until Kellen made me show him and Dwight and Sara what I had done.

"This picture of me doesn't look like an Ugnaught!" said Sara. "It's sweet! Can I keep it? And your smileys are awesome!"

"Yeah, dude, this is stooky stuff," Kellen said. "I'm glad they don't look exactly like the ones in the case file. You've got your own style! And the case file wasn't supposed to turn you into a master. It was just supposed to get you started."

"Yes! Beyond the case file you must go," said Origami Yoda. "Any piece of scrap paper become art it can. Like this one . . . Doodle all over it you must . . ."

Harvey Cunningham II
Ms. Bauer
Third Period

Biography Unit
Assignment 3
Autobiography

I was born in Roanoke but have always lived here.

My parents realized that I was gifted when I was four months old.

My special areas of expertise include math, reading, grammar, spelling, U.S. history, American geography, world history, world geography, movies, science fiction movies, science, biology, entomology (the study of arachnids and insects), advanced chemistry, software development and programming, and, of course, origami.

My origami creations have been featured in the newspaper and have received as many as thirty-seven likes on photowallrus.com.

Currently a seventh grader, I am already taking several college-level web classes and performing exceptionally well in them.

In the future, I think my greatest difficulty will be in deciding which one of my many talents I should pursue as a career.

Then one day I can write another autobiography, which will be a bestseller and will give me a chance to share my knowledge and ideas with the world.

"An important journey you have begun. Complete is your training, but forever will your skills improve," said Origami Yoda. "Cut off your Padawan braid you may."

"Uh . . . I don't have a Padawan braid," I said. "You made me shave my head, remember?"

"Right, yeah, oh . . . ," said Origami Yoda. "Anyway . . ."

"Beep blee-beep," said Kellen, and I thought he had gone crazy, until I realized he was holding Art2 and C-3PO.

"Well done, sir!" said C-3PO. "Might I suggest that the next things you make are some legs for me? It's really quite dreadful without them!"

"Maybe we should tape you onto the back of the Fortune Wookiee," said Sara. "That way you can reenact the last half of *The Empire Strikes Back*!"

"Oh no!" yelled C-3PO/Kellen. "Not that flea-bitten fur ball again! Legs would be quite preferable!"

"But there weren't any instructions!" I said.

"Beep whistle!" went Art2.

"Okay, okay," I said, "I'll figure it out myself!"

"Yes!" said Origami Yoda. "Doodling, folding, and experimenting you must continue. Mistakes will you make, but better and more powerful you will become. That is the way of the Jedi Doodler . . . Finished you may be, but only begun you have."

Harvey's Comment

Well, that was annoying. By the way, has anybody seen my homework for Ms. Bauer's class? I have to turn it in in five minutes!

Tommy's Comment: No comment.

TOMMY AND KELLEN'S BIBLIOGRAPHY

BY TOMMY AND KELLEN

Here are some of the books we used for inspiration, reference, and learning to draw/fold in the first place:

More *Star Wars* Stuff to Make:
Star Wars Origami (Chris Alexander)
The Star Wars Craft Book (Bonnie Burton)
Star Wars Folded Flyers (Ben Harper & *Klutz*)

How to Draw:
Ed Emberly's Drawing Book: Make a World, Ed Emberly's Big Green Book, and a bunch more (Ed Emberly)
Animation (Preston Blair)

How to Fold:
Any origami book you can get your hands on! (Robert Lang, John Montroll, Won Park, and many more!)

Reference:
The Illustrated Star Wars Universe (Ralph McQuarrie and Kevin Anderson)

Millennium Falcon: A 3-D Owner's Guide (Ryder Windham, Chris Trevas, Chris Reiff)
The Making of Star Wars (J. W. Rinzler)
Star Wars: Head to Head (Pablo Hidalgo)
Star Wars: The Visual Dictionary (DK)
Star Wars: The Clone Wars Visual Guide (DK)
Star Wars: Character Encylopedia (DK)
Star Wars: The Clone Wars Character Encyclopedia (DK)

Stooky:
Star Wars: A Galactic Pop-Up Adventure and *Star Wars: A Pop-Up Guide to the Galaxy* (Matthew Reinhart)

Healthy:
Booger-Free You, Booger-Free Me! (Brian "Mr. Good Clean Fun" Compton)

Dwight says this is the book that got him started in the first place: *Curious George Rides a Bike* (H. A. Rey). I know it doesn't sound like an origami book, but it is, sorta!

And, even though they are movies and TV shows and not books: *The Phantom Menace, Attack of the Clones, THE CLONE WARS*!!!! (the television series), *Revenge of the Sith, A New Hope, The Empire Strikes Back,* and *Return of the Jedi*

ABOUT THE AUTHOR

Tom Angleberger is the author of the *New York Times* bestselling Origami Yoda series, which includes *The Strange Case of Origami Yoda*, *Darth Paper Strikes Back*, and *The Secret of the Fortune Wookiee*. He is also the author of *Fake Mustache* and *Horton Halfpott*, an Edgar Award nominee. Visit him online at www.origamiyoda.com. Tom lives in the Appalachian Mountains of Virginia with his wife, author-illustrator Cece Bell, who taught him how to draw dogs.

This book was designed by Melissa J. Arnst and art directed by Chad W. Beckerman. Twenty fonts were used to bring this book to life, including the brand new font ANGLEBERGER! The main text is set in 10-point Lucida Sans Typewriter. The display typeface is ERASER. Tommy's comments are set in Kienan, and Harvey's comments are set in Good Dog. The hand lettering on the cover was done by Jason Rosenstock.

BEEP!
OH, YES, ARTZ... I LOVE A HAPPY ENDING, TOO!
8

MAY THE FOLDS BE WITH YOU!

READ ALL OF THE BOOKS IN TOM ANGLEBERGER'S BESTSELLING ORIGAMI YODA SERIES.

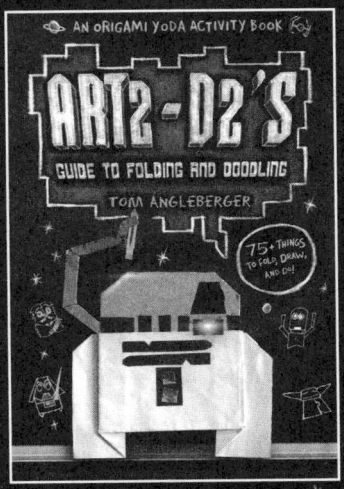

www.origamiyoda.com

SEND AUTHOR FAN MAIL TO:
Amulet Books, Attn: Marketing, 115 West 18th Street, New York, NY 10011.
Or e-mail marketing@abramsbooks.com. All mail will be forwarded.

Amulet Books
An imprint of ABRAMS
WWW.AMULETBOOKS.COM

KEEP READING BOOKS BY BESTSELLING AUTHOR TOM ANGLEBERGER!